The Demon Football Manager

Martin Smith

ISBN: 1517144620
ISBN-13: 978-1517144623

For Mum, Dad, Nicola and David.

CONTENTS

ACKNOWLEDGMENTS

I could not have written The Demon Football Manager without a number of people who gave their time to get involved in the Charlie Fry adventure.
In no particular order, they are:
Fellow Evertonian Brian Amey, who brought Chell Di Santos to life with such distinction on the cover.
Trying to convey evil in an image is always a challenge, but Brian grasped a true understanding of the menacing title character with real flair.
Eagle-eyed Richard Wayte kindly gave up his time to proofread The Demon Football Manager – even though he doesn't like football.
My niece Lucy Smith easily wrote the most engaging and informative review of the Football Boy Wonder via text message. Her words of encouragement were a true inspiration when penning the sequel.
Finally, thank you to all of you who have enjoyed Charlie's journey to date. We go again.

1. HOPES AND HEADLINES

The website flashed up in front of their eyes.

"There," pointed Joe Foster, unable to hide his excitement at the headline in the middle of the tablet's screen.

"Hall Park Boy Wonder Strikes Again!"
By Andrew Hallmaker.

Joe nudged his friend in the ribs: "Click on it!"

Charlie Fry did as his friend asked, his heart beating like a drum.

Seconds later the article popped up and the two boys leaned forward to read the match report from their game the night before.

Charlie shuffled on the couch before plunging into the article.

"Hall Park's Academy Under-13s won their final pre-season friendly 8-0 last night, thanks to an outstanding display from youngster Charlie Fry."

Charlie's cheeks went red.

The Crickledon Telegraph always seemed to be writing about him at the moment – he wasn't used to the limelight.

The story continued:

"Hunsbury Lakes simply had no answer for the superb footballing display produced by Barney Payne's exciting team.

"Captained by impressive goalkeeping prospect Joe Foster, Hall Park scored twice in the first ten minutes and never looked like losing.

"This was – in the main – thanks to star striker Fry, who scored yet another hat-trick.

"The goals took Fry's pre-season total to 27, which is a new record for Hall Park. He is a player of undisputed quality."

The boys skimmed through the article, flickering over the descriptions of last night's goals.

Both were eagerly looking for same thing – the player ratings.

Charlie scanned through the names. His appeared at the very bottom – with a man-of-the-match star alongside it.

"Charlie FRY: 10."

Joe smiled and lightly punched his buddy on the arm: "I kept a clean sheet and even get an assist and I only get a nine! I'll beat you one day, Fry!"

Tongue-tied with shyness, Charlie was unsure what to say to his best friend. The praise was almost embarrassing.

The Telegraph kept giving him man of the match.

This was the fifth time this month – and the season hadn't even started.

"I ... er ... am sorry. You deserve credit too, Joe."

Joe laughed: "Charlie, you scored a hat-trick! Again!

"I'm teasing you, you silly devil. You need to stop taking it so seriously!"

Charlie grinned at Joe, pushing the short brown hair out of his eyes.

He spluttered a little; it was his lungs giving him a little reminder that he still needed to do his daily physio.

"Charlie, I heard that."

His mum Molly appeared in the doorway looking sternly at her eldest child.

"It's time for Joe to go, I think. It's a big day tomorrow for both of you."

Joe took the blatant hint.

He jumped up from the couch, moved towards the front door and began pulling his scuffed trainers on.

"No problem, Molly. Thanks for having me.

"Charlie, I'll knock for you about 7.30am. Okay?"

Joe didn't wait for an answer.

He gave the Fry family a cheerful wave goodbye as he let himself out, and closed the door behind him with a bang.

Charlie swallowed and realised his throat was dry.

He shuffled the tablet off his lap and scowled at his mum, who watched him head upstairs to begin his breathing exercises.

Having cystic fibrosis was such a drag.

Why couldn't he be like everyone else?

Charlie shook his head angrily as he moved towards his bedroom.

No, he had never ever thought like that – being negative was pointless.

Something in the back of his mind told him it was the nerves.

They had been slowly building up inside him over the past few weeks.

Tomorrow was the big day.

They were starting secondary school.

He had spent almost every waking moment of the summer holidays playing or reading about football – it had been brilliant.

But he couldn't ignore it any longer.

He was going to a new school.

And the thought of such a big change made his stomach flip.

Charlie flopped on to his Blues' bed and positioned himself to begin the exercises that helped him stay out of hospital.

He wondered if anyone at his new school would know that he played for Hall Park. Unlikely, he thought.

How many people actually read the Telegraph or attended youth matches for the team?

The club was popular, of course, but that didn't mean people at school would know about him or Joe.

Besides, Charlie was still unsure if he wanted them to know who he was or not.

He liked hanging round with Peter and Joe – and he absolutely loved all the football.

However this 'Football Boy Wonder' nickname was a little silly.

It sounded like he was the next England captain or something.

He hadn't even played for Hall Park in a real

match yet!

And no-one – apart from his closest friends – knew about his big secret: the magic power that had made him such a footballing superstar.

He smiled to himself.

No-one would be finding out either.

That was one secret that was staying well and truly buried.

Charlie sighed, unable to get rid of the butterflies that fluttered away merrily in his tummy.

He was going to a new school and set for a fresh start – without those idiot school bullies hounding every move.

So why did he feel terrified?

2. A FRESH START

Charlie did not need to worry.

It turned out that almost everyone at Crickledon Fields Secondary School knew exactly who he was.

And it seemed like every student in his year wanted to come over, introduce themselves to him and shake his hand.

They'd all been reading the Telegraph's website over the summer, soaking up the stories about the town's new footballing wonder kid.

Charlie smiled and shook everyone's hand, unused to being centre of attention. Joe and their other best friend Peter Bell flanked him closely but it wasn't needed.

No-one was mean or unfriendly.

Many of the pupils just wanted to go home and proudly tell their parents they'd met the Football Boy Wonder.

Lunch break was nearly over by the time the three friends found a quiet corner to gobble down their packed lunches.

They were starving – even Charlie for once – because their new lunch break started almost an hour later than it did at their old school.

It felt odd to be eating so late in the day.

They did not speak at first – too busy shoving their sandwiches, crisps and fruit into their mouths as though they'd never eaten before.

Charlie didn't eat all of his packed lunch but it was still more than he'd eaten in a long time.

The boy looked at his friends, who were still munching away.

They were all wearing red ties for the first time – each of them was dressed in new black shoes, black trousers and white shirts.

Charlie's tummy butterflies had disappeared as the morning had gone on.

He had not slept well and had been unable to eat breakfast before Joe came knocking on his door.

His mum and dad understood, smiled supportively and did not tell him off about eating for once.

Both of them gave him a big hug as he left, despite his protests.

Charlie guessed they too had been young once – probably a very long, long time ago.

After stopping to call for Peter, they had arrived at the school 30 minutes early and followed signs that directed new arrivals to meet in the hall.

It slowly filled up with plenty of familiar faces.

Then the students were put into form groups.

Charlie and Peter were put in the same tutor group but Joe unfortunately had been placed in one of the others.

It was one of those things.

The situation was only for form time though.

They would still see each in most of their lessons and during breaks.

Each pupil had been given a timetable of subjects and a map to help guide them around the huge site.

Peter and Charlie had already managed to get lost twice.

Joe, it seemed, already knew his way around the school's labyrinth of corridors and classrooms as if he'd been here for years.

The teachers had been friendly and understanding – even when kids turned up late. It was their first day after all.

Joe looked up, and caught Charlie staring into space as he recalled the morning's events. It had been like a whirlwind.

"Hey Fry-inho. Are you still dreaming about that hat-trick?"

Peter chuckled at Joe's banter before shuffling in his seat.

It had been three weeks since Peter's cast had been removed but his leg – badly hurt in the Hall Park summer trials by that moron Adam Knight – still caused him pain.

Charlie admired his friend's spirit.

Peter, who played brilliantly that day until Knight's terrible tackle saw him stretchered off, had not been able to play since.

But his friend never moaned though or complained about his bad luck.

He simply smiled and told Joe and Charlie that he would be back soon enough.

Hall Park bosses had promised him a place on the academy squad – although Peter would not be playing for the first team for a while

Recovering from a broken leg was a long process and could not be rushed.

Peter did not need his crutches any more but running was still not possible.

Doctors said it would be a couple of weeks before he could start running again. Playing football would follow soon after.

Peter looked at Charlie too, his eyes still twinkling with laughter.

"Did you leave your tongue back at primary school, Fry?"

Charlie smiled. Peter and Joe were his best friends – they teased him often but it was all in good spirits.

"Get lost.

"I guess...."

His words tailed off as he considered what he was wanted to say.

Peter and Joe stayed silent and patiently waited for their friend to finish his sentence.

Charlie closed his eyes and took a deep breath.

He blurted the words out: "I guess after everything that has happened, it feels like a fresh start.

"I feel like I finally belong."

He opened his eyes to look at his friends, expecting some sort of witty response from the pair but it did not arrive.

They were both looking somewhere over his right shoulder, faces aghast.

"Awwww.

"You hear that, boys?

"Little Fry baby thinks he's going to be happy here.

"Isn't that sweet?"

Charlie's heart sunk.

He knew that sneer only too well.

Standing only a few metres behind him was a grinning Adam Knight.

3. AN OLD ENEMY

Charlie turned slowly to face the awful bully who had made his life a misery throughout primary school.

For once Adam was alone, his cronies nowhere to be seen.

He stood lurking in the doorway that led into the small concrete courtyard where the boys had been eating lunch.

With a familiar smirk, he spoke in a spiteful voice.

"Surprised ladies?"

Charlie sighed.

As far as he knew, Adam had been joining another secondary school.

He had been booted out of the Hall Park trials after his horror tackle on Peter so at least they no longer had to endure him on the pitch.

It had meant they had barely seen him all summer apart from the bully flinging insults on the odd occasion they saw him at The Rec.

Without the bully's taunts, Charlie's confidence had flourished both on and off the pitch.

He used to think about school with dread but recently he had looked forward to each day with excitement.

The Football Boy Wonder was loving life. Times had changed.

But now Adam was back.

Charlie scowled at the shaven haired thug, who seemed to have grown even larger during the summer break.

"What are you doing here, Knight?"

Joe's voice boomed across the courtyard as he and Peter stepped either side of Charlie to face their enemy together.

Adam wore trainers and his tie was already half undone. He looked like he'd just dragged himself out of bed.

"Haven't you heard? I'm part of this school now.

"Turns out Choldington Boys' School wasn't the right place for me – so my parents decided to send me here instead."

The bully's upper lip turned up in a sneer.

"It's a real dump but it'll do, I suppose."

His eyes stopped on Peter and the evil grin spread over his face again.

"How's the leg, Belly?" he gloated.

"Fine thanks, Knight," Peter fired back hotly.

"It'll be even better when I'm playing for Hall Park next season. You didn't quite make it did you?"

Adam shrugged.

"I was obviously too good for them. If people like him," – he nodded in Charlie's direction – "can get a game then the standard is way too low."

It was Peter's turn to mock.

"Ha ha ha. Yes, of course, I remember now. You

were nearly crying when you got sent off.

"Bye-bye to your football career. Cheats never win, Addy, my old chum."

Joe and Charlie laughed loudly at Peter's taunts, delighted to see Adam finally getting a taste of his own medicine.

Adam though did not respond.

He smiled, a sickly sweet ear-to-ear grin that stopped the chuckles.

"Sometimes you need to put your foot in and make a tackle.

"I can't help it if my foot accidentally slipped and broke your leg, can I?

"Anyway, some clubs can see real talent – unlike those morons at Hall Park.

"That's why I'll be playing for Colts next season. They've even named me as captain so we'll see each other again on the football pitch real soon."

Thrapborough Colts.

They were Hall Park's biggest rivals, easily the strongest team in the league.

They were well known for poaching other team's top players – even taking some of Hall Park's star players in recent years.

Surely he was joking?

If not, he would be playing against them this season ... with the top side in the league.

Adam looked at Charlie with a threatening expression: "Watch out for your bony little legs, Football Boy Wonder, or you may end up like your little girlfriend."

The thug winked triumphantly, turned and left the three boys staring at the space where he had been standing.

For a moment they were speechless.

It was Joe who broke the awkward silence, slapping both of his friends on their shoulders.

"Let's forget about that pilchard.

"We've only got one more day at school and then it is Hall Park debut day."

Their first match against Choldington Weavers was scheduled for Saturday lunchtime.

To no-one's surprise, Joe had already been named captain for Hall Park Rovers.

The rest of the team would be named on the day of the match.

He may be known as the Football Boy Wonder but Charlie could barely contain his excitement at the thought of taking part in a competitive match.

Saturday was the day he had always dreamed about, although his dreams had been more like nightmares in recent weeks.

He dreaded waking up one morning and finding his targeting power had disappeared overnight.

It was still there, of course, the black shape ready to spring into life whenever he stepped on to the pitch.

Charlie said a silent prayer to that freak thunderbolt for about the thousandth time.

He nodded to Joe and picked up his school bag as the bell rang to signal the end of lunch.

But there was another feeling too – Charlie felt tired of having to put up with the childish insults from numbskulls like Knight.

Despite Charlie's previous high hopes of a fresh start, it seemed the bully would continue to be pain in the neck.

He would just have to grin and bear it.

But Joe was right: they had other things to think about.

Hall Park needed them.

4. HALL PARK

Charlie and Joe stood on the cracked pavement and looked up in awe at the ancient stand looming over them.

The pair had been to Hall Park many times before but this was different.

They had always been part of the crowd cheering on the first team as their heroes tried to get into the football league.

Now they would be out on the pitch instead.

It was a completely different challenge.

Charlie shielded his eyes from the bright Saturday morning sunshine muttering that the ground had never looked so big.

Joe agreed with a murmur but both were lost in their own thoughts.

They had arrived an hour early – the first game of the Hall Park Under-13 season was due to kick off at 1pm.

It was September but the autumn day was boiling hot – perfect weather to play football.

When the boys caught sight of the ground on match days, it always gave them goose bumps with anticipation.

Yet today was a hundred times worse.

To people who did not like or understand soccer, the Hall Park ground was not a pretty picture.

For starters no-one with any sense would describe it as "modern".

A two-tier stand with 50 seats in the upper part had been built alongside one of the touchlines.

There was old-fashioned terracing in the lower area – space for 150 people to stand – behind the two dugouts for the managers and subs.

A small doorway led to the Hall Park changing rooms and the social club underneath the stand.

The rest of the pitch was surrounding by railings and concrete terraces for supporters to watch the games from.

Swanky houses with long gardens overlooked the pitch at one end, their residents given a prime spot to watch the football from upstairs windows.

A friend at their old primary school – his name was Darren but people called him 'Mudder' for reasons Charlie had never discovered – lived in one of them.

It meant Mudder was able to watch every Hall Park game for free from his bedroom window.

Charlie, Joe and Peter had talked excitedly about those houses many times.

They were expensive – huge houses with sweeping driveways and immaculate gardens.

To the boys, those houses were everything.

And, when they grew up, they all wanted to own one.

If it ever happened, they could all watch Hall Park's games whenever they wished – for free. It was a dream they had shared for years.

At the opposite end of the ground from Mudder's house, a row of conifer trees stood behind the goal.

They were enormous, giving fans little room to pass each other on the tight terracing.

It may not have been much to some but it was the boys' very own Theatre of Dreams.

To play on the Hall Park pitch in a real match would fulfil a lifetime ambition for Charlie and Joe.

Of course, the Under-13s' academy match would not attract a big crowd.

Proud parents for both of the teams, a few club officials and one or two die-hard Hall Park fans would make up the audience.

Nonetheless this was their big day.

The sun slipped behind one of the few clouds in the blue sky, the shadow breaking the strange spell that had fallen over the boys.

Joe nudged Charlie's arm.

"Come on Boy Wonder. We've got a game to win."

The goalkeeper slung his bag over his shoulder, marched towards the double doors in front of them, yanked them open and ushered his friend through.

Framed photos of Hall Park's previous captains and triumphs hung on the walls in the narrow corridor.

Joe had been a ball-boy for Hall Park last season – much to Charlie and Peter's envy – so he knew where he was going.

Charlie followed his friend, his eyes wide open.

They passed the social club bar where they could

hear a handful of people chatting away.

The corridor swung right and immediately two doors stood in front of them. Big letters hung on each door.

The right one said: "AWAY."

The left one – with the Hall Park badge positioned in pride of place – said: "HOME."

Charlie felt a shiver of excitement as he looked at the badge.

This was really happening, after all.

Joe opened the changing room door and they walked in, ready for the biggest game of their lives.

5. CHELL DI SANTOS

A dozen faces turned to greet them as they strolled into the changing room, allowing the door to slam behind them.

It fell quiet as the biggest lad in the room stepped away from the crowd gathered around a piece of paper pinned on the far wall.

Striding towards the newcomers, Brian Bishop eyed the pair up and down before breaking into a huge smile.

"All right, Skip?"

The striker, whose shaven head still revealed a hint of his ginger locks, high-fived Joe before he grabbed Charlie in a crushing bear hug.

"And how's the Boy Wonder today?"

"Gerrrofff!" said Charlie, laughing as he fought to untangle himself.

Bishop was Charlie's strike partner up front, with Peter jokingly describing him as "The Bodyguard".

He was a tough lad but a talented footballer too and he had become a good friend over the summer months.

Finally Bishop let Charlie out of his grip and stood aside so the pair could get closer to the team sheet on the noticeboard.

It read:

Hall Park Under-13s v Choldington Weavers Under-13s

Saturday, September 6. Kick-off : 1pm.

Manager: Barney Payne.

1. *Joe Foster. (C)*
2. *Seamus Houseman.*
3. *Billy Walton.*
4. *Manny Serbe.*
5. *Simon Sherwood.*
6. *James Hart.*
7. *Aaron Underwood.*
8. *Charlie Fry.*
9. *Brian Bishop.*
10. *Shivander Silvio.*
11. *Andre Jones.*

Subs: Henry Speed, Ed Raith, Johnny Somore, Perc Zolyski, Tim Wilson, Tom Davies, Paulo Keay.

Charlie swallowed hard as he studied the team sheet.

Deep down he guessed he would start.

His form during pre-season had been very impressive – the paper had even said so.

But, as ever in Charlie's mind, there was a nagging

doubt.

His lungs were in good shape, the warm summer months and daily exercise helping to keep his cystic fibrosis stable.

He had not needed hospital treatment for almost six months.

As if to remind himself of his current good health, Charlie took a deep breath and held it.

His airways – so often rattling and oozing full of sticky gunge – were clear.

It felt great.

And reassuringly, the target was floating harmlessly around his vision, lazily waiting for its moment of glory to arrive.

It would soon be put to good use.

Charlie edged away from the team sheet to allow others to see whether they had made the starting line-up and followed Joe to an empty space near the door.

Charlie glanced around the room as he moved. Something wasn't right. Charlie did a quick head count.

There were only 18 of the squad here.

He checked his watch – only a few minutes remained until they were due to meet up.

The familiar faces of Manny and Paulo wandered through the door as Charlie sat down, making their way straight to the team sheet.

But that was it.

There had been almost 40 players named in the squad after the Hall Park summer camp.

Where was everyone else?

Charlie leaned over to whisper in Joe's ear.

"Where's Mike? Where is everyone else?"

Mike Parson had played alongside them at the Hall

Park trials and had been with them at almost every training session since.

He was another one of their group – and a decent defender too.

Charlie continued: "They can't all be late surely?"

Joe scanned the room, shrugged and raised his eyebrows.

"I have no idea. I…."

Joe's voice tailed off as Barney Payne – the Hall Park manager – entered the changing room.

The veteran coach shuffled between the excited players and stood in the middle of the room.

You could have heard a pin drop as the boss began to speak.

"Gentlemen, well done for arriving on time.

"The pre-match warm-up starts in ten minutes.

"No doubt, you've seen the team sheet. Good luck to those in the starting line-up.

"However I would like to remind you this is a team game.

"Everyone will get a run out today so I expect all of you to be ready when your chance arrives.

"If you impress in today's game, your name could well be in the starting line-up next week.

"Remember we win and lose as a team.

"The subs are just as important as the starting 11. Now get changed, and let's start the season in style."

A cheer went round the changing room as the boys dived into their bags to pull their new Hall Park kits and boots on.

Joe, however, put his hand up.

"Er, Gaffer?"

Barney looked at the burly goalkeeper, a small smile forming around the edge of his mouth.

"Yes, Joe?"

"Where is everyone else?"

The room fell quiet again as the team waited for Barney's answer.

Obviously Joe and Charlie were not the only ones to notice their missing teammates.

Barney chewed his lip thoughtfully before answering.

He pushed his messy white hair out of his eyes and spoke clearly.

"That's a good point, Skipper. As you know, we had a large pool of talent this season compared with other years.

"We narrowed down the total number of players to just under 40 but that's still far too big for the league rules.

"So we've divided up the squad into two teams.

"You are Hall Park Rovers.

"The other team is called Hall Park Magpies.

"They'll play in the same division but wear our away colours and will play their games at Manor Park. Has anyone got any questions?"

Bishop's hand shot up.

"Who will manage them?"

Barney smiled weakly. "I will."

Bishop looked confused: "You surely can't manage both teams though, Gaffer?"

"No, you're right. You boys will be getting a new manager. I'm looking after you today before the new man starts next week."

A deathly silence fell over the room.

The team looked shell-shocked.

Barney's team talks could be a little confusing and he was always forgetting their names but he was honest, fair and a football expert.

And now they were losing him – just one game into the season.

Alarmed at the sudden turn of events Joe stood up: "So who is going to be our manager then?"

Barney nodded towards the door.

"Here he is now."

The timing could not have been better. The changing room door flew open with force, the handle almost striking Charlie in the face.

A tall man stood in the doorway, dressed entirely in black and wearing a long winter coat despite the mild temperatures.

His dark hair was immaculately combed into a side parting and his blue eyes were like lasers as they swept the room.

When he spoke, his voice was low but razor sharp.

"My name is Chell Di Santos. I am your manager now.

"You will call me 'Boss'.

"Understand this: I am a winner and I do not tolerate losers."

Charlie felt the manager's glare settle on him, sending butterflies through his stomach.

Satisfied he had their complete attention, Di Santos continued: "Nothing else matters. Football is everything.

"Football is our lives. We live to win.

"If you think like me and are prepared to work harder than you have ever worked, we will get along fine.

"If not, you won't last very long at Hall Park."

His eyes swept around the room again, almost urging someone in the team to disagree with him.

Yet no-one said a word or moved a muscle.

With the clear threat hanging in the air, the newcomer turned and departed leaving a shocked changing room behind him.

After several seconds of silence Barney cleared his throat and addressed the team again.

"Mr Di Santos is a qualified coach and is very highly rated.

"He has won numerous trophies with some of the leading academy sides in Spain in recent years.

"The club have brought him in specifically to manage your age group due to the extremely … rare talent we have available in this year group."

Charlie could feel the others looking at him but he kept his stare fixed on Barney.

He thought the old coach looked sad in some way, perhaps even a little worried.

Barney blew out his cheeks and spoke again: "Okay, enough talking.

"Let's get out there. We've got a game to win."

6. DEBUT

Choldington Weavers were big.

They were not big as a club.

They always seemed to be stuck in mid-table – a side that Hall Park confidently expected to beat every season.

But the Weavers' Under-13s players were huge in size.

Every player wearing Weavers' bright green kit towered above Charlie, he did not even come up to the shoulder of the two burly centre-backs.

Even Bishop and Joe looked small against them.

To the small crowd gathering in the main stand, it looked a complete mismatch.

Both the teams were out on the pitch waiting for the referee to carry out the coin-toss.

"Men against boys," muttered Ed Ashby, who had looked after the Hall Park ground for the past 30 years.

A few people standing nearby nodded in agreement with Ed's verdict.

The old groundsman lived and breathed football. He claimed to know the Beautiful Game inside out.

Several parents already looked sick with worry – and the game hadn't started yet.

Pleased to have an interested audience to listen to his views, Ed continued: "Still we have the Boy Wonder, don't we?

"He's a hell of a player. You should have seen him on the pre-season tour.

"Fry is electric. Give him the ball and he'll make something happen.

"I've seen thousands of players come and go during my time.

"He's better than all of them. Charlie Fry is something special."

A woman wearing a green Weavers shirt standing next to him turned to face Ed: "Which one is this Boy Wonder kid?"

Ed laughed.

"He's the little lad talking to our manager.

"Don't worry though, he may be tough to spot at the moment but you'll soon be sick of the sight of him!"

The woman chewed her lip deep in thought.

"Is he really that good?"

Ed grinned and wiped the sweat out of his eyes with a grass-stained finger.

"Lady, the Boy Wonder is going to play in the Premier League. Not only that, I think he'll captain England."

The Weavers fan laughed but cut her chuckle short when she realised Ed was being completely serious.

She turned away from the conversation, talking about what she'd just been told in hushed tones to the man standing next to her.

The ref blew the whistle and the two captains jogged towards the centre circle.

Joe and the Weavers' skipper shook hands and the teams swapped ends after the away captain called the coin-toss correctly.

Ed watched the two teams of players moving before glancing around at the crowd again.

"I've never seen so many people here for an Under 13s game.

"We normally get a maximum of 50 people. I reckon there are almost 150 here today. I wonder who they've come here to see?"

As part of his regular routine Joe had checked the net, both of the goalposts and marked the centre of his goal with his studs.

The goalkeeper clapped his hands to encourage the Hall Park team as they took up their positions ready for kick-off.

Charlie bounced on the spot on the edge of the centre circle, a bundle of nervous energy.

Ed noticed a group of kids unravelling a huge banner.

In large bold letters it simply said:

"Charlie Fry = Football Legend."

The groundsman snorted: "Not quite yet!

"This is all the Telegraph's fault.

"The boy needs some time and space.

"Instead that newspaper has hyped him up and now we've got this sort of nonsense with banner and blooming fan clubs."

One of the parents leaning on a railing nearby

turned to face the groundsman.

He piped up: "Hang on, a minute ago you were claiming Charlie to be the best footballer we've ever had!

"Everyone is excited about Charlie – and rightly so!

"But don't blame the paper when you're just as bad!"

Ed huffed, unhappy that someone had disagreed with him.

He remembered he had work to do and moved off towards the far end of the ground, chuntering to himself about people who did not understand the game.

Chell Di Santos silently watched the groundsman depart.

He was wearing dark sunglasses so no-one could see his eyes and had not moved a muscle during the recent conversation.

But he had not missed a word.

The manager's hands had been tucked inside his thick coat but his pasty white hand emerged, holding a thin pencil and a small notebook.

None of the crowd knew that he was the new boss of Rovers' exciting Under-13s Academy side, not even Ed.

They would find out soon enough though.

Taking a quick look at the banner displayed in the stand, he began to scribble some notes into his pad.

Di Santos's gaze returned to the pitch as the game kicked off.

His blue eyes – hidden from view of everyone else by the dark sunglasses – were fixed on one person alone.

Charlie Fry.
The Hall Park Wonder Kid.

7. GOALS GALORE

Charlie had been too on edge to eat any breakfast.

He had wanted to vomit all morning.

The nerves, as ever, were not far away. The target floated around his eyesight, all set for action when called upon.

He swallowed mouthfuls of air as he waited for Weavers to get the game – and the season – under way.

The whistle blew. They were finally away.

Almost immediately Weavers' tactics were revealed.

They had one clear advantage – their size – and they did not intend to waste it.

The green shirts were intent on pumping the ball high into Hall Park's penalty area and hoping their lanky strikers would do the rest.

It was not pretty but it was effective.

They pushed the home side back straight away with Seamus – the only one of Adam's gang of bullies who had made the Hall Park Rovers' cut – sent flying into the turf the first minute.

Seamus got to his feet gingerly, spitting out strands of grass as he did so. He was not used to be being bowled over.

For the first five minutes, Charlie was a virtual spectator.

He had not even touched the ball.

He was being man-marked by Weavers' strapping captain Will, who was never more than two steps behind the Boy Wonder.

Bishop had tried to win several loose balls but had come off distinctly second best against his own marker.

It meant the ball was constantly being returned towards Hall Park's goal.

However as Weavers began to press harder and grab the opening goal, they left the back door open.

Seamus – who after his initial tumble was having a storming game at centre-back – had headed the ball out for a corner.

Encouraged by their dominant start to the match, both of Weavers' central defenders moved forward to attack the corner kick.

Bishop loitered on the edge of his own penalty area completely unmarked.

Charlie stood in the centre circle, watched closely by the two covering opposition defenders.

The in-swinging corner flew into the box from the left-hand side.

Green shirts flew forward to try to meet the tantalising cross but they were frustrated by Joe, who cleanly rose above everyone to punch the ball away from danger.

The clearance fell perfectly for Hall Park.

Bishop gathered the ball, turned and, still completely unmarked, strode towards the Weavers' half.

Charlie had begun to move as soon as Joe had punched the corner clear.

Instinct told him to peel left ensuring the pair of remaining defenders had to split to deal with both threats.

It worked.

One of the Weavers defenders stepped forward to intercept Bishop while the other tracked Charlie's run.

Bishop had spent the summer playing alongside Charlie and the pair had developed a good understanding.

The big striker knew Charlie would wait until the covering defender had almost reached him before moving diagonally right, moving across the width of the pitch.

It would allow Bishop to slip the ball to his strike partner and give him acres of space to run into, created by Charlie's zig-zag movement.

Charlie made his move right on cue and Bishop delivered the pass perfectly into his path.

The Boy Wonder could hear the last defender trying to catch up, caught off guard by his strange movements.

Charlie knew Bishop would now be haring into the free space – it was just a matter of timing the pass back to his unmarked strike partner.

He collected the ball, turned swiftly and … BANG!

The Weavers goalkeeper appeared from nowhere.

He had rushed out of his penalty area and launched into a sliding tackle that cleaned out Charlie and the ball.

The tackle was so hard that the keeper and Charlie tumbled off the pitch, ending up in a heap of arms and legs on the touchline.

The keeper pushed Charlie back down as he got to his feet first.

As he helped Charlie up, he gave the striker a quick wink and whispered: "Not too special then."

Charlie snorted but did not reply.

Banter was all part of the game.

His breathing was ragged and he felt a little weak. Not having eaten earlier now appeared to have been a mistake.

But he forced himself to concentrate.

The ref had awarded a throw-in to Hall Park but no free-kick.

Charlie trotted slowly back into the action and refused to argue with the ref.

He concentrated on breathing steadily, and prepared himself for the next attack.

It came quickly.

Inspired by the sudden counter-attack, Hall Park came alive.

The midfielders began winning tackles, harrying and hassling Weavers into making mistakes and pushing the opposition deeper into their own half.

Charlie was still a little shaky when Hall Park's big chance came.

The striker had not been able to join the attack and was jogging a fair distance behind as Bishop, standing on the penalty spot, volleyed a beauty towards the top corner.

Yet the Weavers goalkeeper – another giant with long shaggy blonde hair – was equal to it once more.

He threw himself to his left-hand side and his long fingers managed to nudge the ball on to the crossbar and out for a corner.

The crowd applauded loudly as they recognised outstanding skills from both players.

Weavers celebrated like they'd won the game, clapping their keeper on the back and whooping with joy.

Their happiness did not last long.

The corner was swung into the box and partially headed clear back towards Rovers' quick winger Shivander 'Shiv' Silvio.

Shiv's second cross was also headed away by a defender; the ball landed at Charlie's feet a couple of metres outside the box.

This time Boy Wonder did not hesitate.

With opposition players rushing to close him down, Charlie flicked his eyes towards the top right-hand corner of the goal.

The black target, which had been floating around pointlessly for the entire game so far, sprang to life as it always did.

It locked into position and flashed green in the blink of an eye.

Knowing exactly where the ball would end up, Charlie smashed it with every ounce of strength he had.

A split second later, the ball crashed into the net via the underside of the crossbar.

The goalkeeper had not even moved.

GOAL!

Charlie did not want to be crushed by his excited teammates like the crazy pile-up at the summer trials.

This time he knew exactly what he wanted to do.

He ran towards the touchline to the spot where his parents were standing.

Followed by the rest of his delirious team, the striker charged straight into his dad with a huge bear hug before the family were engulfed in the team's celebrations.

Even Joe ran from his goal to join them.

As he pulled away from his dad and saw his mum crying with joy, Charlie realised he had fulfilled a lifelong dream.

He had scored for Hall Park in a competitive game, one that actually mattered and would go into the record books.

He had done it.

And the crowd loved it.

Even the Weavers supporters applauded Charlie's strike – a screamer that was already being uploaded to YouTube as the celebrations died down.

Everyone was clapping … except for one person who stood with his hands firmly wedged into his pockets.

His expression barely changed.

The only movement was the frown, which could not be seen by the rest of the crowd, deepened even further.

His eyes absorbed everything from behind the dark sunglasses but did not twinkle with appreciation.

There was not even the smallest sign of a smile on his lips.

Chell Di Santos, it seemed, was not as easily impressed as the rest of the ecstatic Hall Park crowd.

8. UNIMPRESSED

"Foul!"

Bishop cried out as Weavers' captain slid through the back of his legs, a juddering tackle that sent him tumbling.

The referee whistled, placing the ball down for a free kick a couple of metres outside of the Weavers penalty area.

A buzz of excitement travelled round the crowd as Charlie placed the ball down, concentration etched on his face.

Five minutes had gone in the second half.

Hall Park were 2-0 up and the game, so physical at the start, had become little more than a stroll.

Weavers were now so worried about Charlie that two men marked him at all times. It hadn't stopped him scoring again though.

With only seconds to go before half-time Joe spotted Charlie moving away from his marker and booted the ball towards him with a hefty kick.

As the ball hung in the air, Charlie knew exactly what to do.

He glanced towards the Weavers goal, set the target and saw the goalkeeper rushing out at high speed, probably intending to clatter him again.

The first time he'd done it, the 'keeper had surprised Charlie.

Trying to repeat the same trick again was foolish – and made Charlie's task far easier.

Charlie did not even wait for the ball to bounce.

As the ball came down, he simply used his side foot to lob the ball over the oncoming keeper on the volley.

It flew high over the stranded goalkeeper and bounced into the empty net exactly where the target had been placed.

It was the final kick of the first half and it seemed to knock the stuffing out of Weavers.

Two goals down despite dominating a large part of the first half, their players looked beaten as they slumped on the touchline with water and oranges.

Hall Park, meanwhile, had been jubilant.

The crowd was buzzing too.

Standing over the ball ready to take the free-kick Charlie could feel the weight of expectation from the fans.

He looked towards Bishop, who dusted himself down after the foul and lightly nodded before moving away.

Weavers had put five men in the wall to try to stop another Charlie Fry rocket ending up in the back of their net.

Bishop was standing at the end of the wall, generally making himself a nuisance as the defenders tried to jostle him out of the way.

Charlie focused on the ball and carefully took seven paces back.

The ref blew and Charlie began striding towards the ball.

He did not lock the target this time though.

There was no need.

Everyone expected a thunderbolt free-kick and being predictable was not cool.

"To be the best, you need imagination!"

Bishop had drilled that thought into him over and over again throughout the football summer camp.

As Charlie reached the ball, Bishop peeled away from the defensive wall into the empty space behind.

To the surprise of the entire stadium, Charlie did not shoot.

He slipped the ball along the ground to his now unmarked strike partner.

With the ball at his feet and completely free inside the penalty area, Bishop neatly brought the ball under control before dispatching it under the goalkeeper for one of the simplest goals he would ever score.

The crowd erupted into cheers yet again as Weavers' players stood blaming each other for the slap-dash marking.

They weren't the only ones fooled.

Everybody – with the sole exception of Bishop – had been expecting a shot.

As Bishop celebrated with the rest of the team into the corner, Charlie walked slowly back towards the touchline.

He was already exhausted, his hands shaking with tiredness.

The lack of food meant he was now struggling

badly.

"You okay, Charlie?"

Barney sensed the little striker was struggling.

Charlie smiled weakly and picked up his inhaler. He took in two large puffs as the Rovers players began to untangle from the pile-up in the far corner.

But Barney had been a coach for a long time and was not fooled.

He wouldn't take any risks with this special young lad.

A minute later, Charlie's number was called out.

The Boy Wonder was being substituted.

The news of the Hall Park Rovers change was met with groans of disbelief from the jubilant crowd.

Charlie's heart sank as he heard the number eight being called out.

His game was over far too quickly.

It had been brilliant, every single moment of it.

But deep down, he knew Barney had made the right decision.

He could not regain his breath despite the help of his inhaler.

Charlie fought the urge to be sick by swallowing mouthfuls of air. It didn't really help; he needed to sit down and rest.

The crowd rose to their feet as the two-goal hero trudged to the touchline, applause ringing out across the empty stadium.

With blood thundering in his ears, Charlie could barely hear the noise from the crowd.

But he could still make out the chant:

"One Boy Wonder! There's only one Boy Wonder ..."

He smiled awkwardly and waved an arm to the main stand, the unexpected chanting making his cheeks blush.

Even though it was a tad embarrassing, Charlie could almost feel himself grow an extra centimetre and pushed out his chest a fraction more than usual.

People were actually singing his name!

Charlie Fry!

Trudging slowly as he listened to the singing, he shook hands with his replacement Johnny Somore, a skilful striker who was only a fraction taller than Charlie.

The Boy Wonder took a seat on the bench as the coaches and other substitutes took turns to high-five and slap the star striker on the back.

Amid all the fanfare, no-one noticed a member of the crowd slip away.

Chell Di Santos had studied the substitution with cold eyes, his mouth forming a small unpleasant sneer.

He straightened his jacket, turned and departed the stadium without a word as the fans continued to sing Charlie's name.

Di Santos did not look back or bother to see closing stages of the game, which still had more than 30 minutes to play.

The new manager of Hall Park Rovers Under-13s had evidently seen enough.

9. COOPS

The Crickledon Telegraph's match report on the Hall Park Rovers game went live on its website just before 6pm on the same day.

As he had done almost every Saturday during the summer, Charlie sat with his tablet and waited for the paper's website to publish the report.

His heart leapt as the headline finally popped up on his screen.

"Boy Wonder bags double in Hall Park romp"
by Andrew Hallmaker

Wonder kid Charlie Fry scored twice as Hall Park Rovers Academy Under-13s began the new season in style with a 6-1 win against Choldington Weavers.

The youngster – who lit up Rovers' pre-season with a series of sensational strikes – continued his impressive form in the first match of the Academy season.

Choldington began strongly but once Fry got into the game, there was only ever going to be one winner.

This young striker is a footballer with a rare talent.

His first goal was an unstoppable thunderbolt, the second was a perfect lob over the onrushing goalkeeper.

Hall Park has a rare diamond on its hands.

Fry – who made the third for fellow striker Brian Bishop with a cleverly worked free-kick – will no doubt be soon compared to Johnny Cooper.

Except – despite his young age – Fry is a better player already. He really is something special....

Charlie's mouth dropped open. He stopped reading the match report and put his hand to his mouth in shock.

Was this journalist guy for real?

Johnny Cooper was universally recognised as Hall Park's greatest ever player, an attacking full back who had played in the Championship for the Dons.

Small but fearsome in the tackle, 'Coops' was Hall Park's favourite son – often touted as the club's own David Beckham.

He had played 78 times for the club and many of Hall Park's supporters had predicted an England call-up in the early days of his career.

Coops never managed to make the grade for England but had enjoyed a decent professional football career for more than a decade.

Now the paper was confidently predicting Charlie was going to be better than Coops – despite the fact that he was only 11!

This was bizarre.

He had only played one competitive game and a handful of friendlies for the academy.

Why were they so obsessed with him?

Deep down, he knew the answer.

Goals.

He was a goal machine.

The magic target in his mind made him stand out on a football field above all the others and people were beginning to take notice.

Charlie squirmed uncomfortably in his seat.

Should he tell someone about the magical gift that had made him unstoppable at football? Was he cheating in some way?

However would anyone actually believe him if he did decide to tell them about the magic target that people used in flick football apps?

The whole situation was pretty far-fetched after all.

The lightning bolt, the football app, the floating target ... it sounded like a small boy's dream. Except this was no dream, it was real.

Peter and Joe knew, of course, but they were his best friends.

And even they had taken some convincing when he had plucked up the courage to confess earlier in the summer.

To be fair, Charlie didn't understand it completely himself.

But he did know this: wherever he placed the target with his mind, the ball would end up.

All he had to do was decide upon how hard to kick it and the rest was already taken care of.

Hours of practice had helped him hone his skills using the target, and now he was reaping the rewards.

People would think he was crazy, and loads of pompous doctors would probably try to cart him off to a scary hospital somewhere.

Hospital. Again.

That thought ended any doubts Charlie had.

He saw the inside of plenty of hospitals with his cystic fibrosis treatment and didn't want to spend more time in them.

He shook his head.

That lightning strike had nearly killed him but instead it opened up a whole new world.

He had no idea how the app's flick football target had become lodged inside his brain and, to be truthful, he no longer cared.

It was there – and it did not appear to be going anywhere.

And that suited him just fine.

No, he needed to keep this secret hidden locked up deep inside of him.

After all, he had a football career to concentrate on.

Charlie had read enough.

He shut the tablet down and walked over towards his nebuliser to begin his evening medication.

He was Charlie Fry – a footballer and a schoolboy. The others could talk and get excited about his goals.

The Boy Wonder just wanted to get out on the pitch and play football.

10. FOOTBALL CELEBRITY

If Charlie hoped he could keep a low profile at school on Monday morning after his Hall Park heroics, then he was mistaken.

Everyone seemed to have read the Telegraph's report.

Some of the school kids – even older ones – had labelled Charlie 'Messi' with many others asking to take selfies with him.

Charlie endured the attentions of the huge crowds of well-wishers with good grace, being polite and agreeing to all requests.

Peter and Joe hung back from chaos, yet still close enough to be on hand in the unlikely event that anything got out of hand.

They found the whole situation hilarious.

And it wasn't only the pupils who had become members of the Charlie Fry fan club.

Charlie was even given a round of applause at the lower school assembly with assistant headteacher Benny Hammitt hailing him as the town's new football superstar.

With his face and neck turning crimson, Charlie was invited to go on stage and shake Mr Hammitt's hand in front of hundreds of students.

It was not until home time that Charlie, Joe and Peter finally got a chance to talk each other without other people listening.

It had been a crazy day and Charlie was worn out.

Walking back through The Rec towards home, Peter piped up first: "Well, knowing a celebrity is a lot less fun than I thought it would be."

Charlie shoved him playfully in the back.

"Shut up."

Peter jogged a couple of paces ahead and turned to face his two friends, walking backwards along the wide path.

"Only kidding. Anyway did you hear about the big news about Magpies?

"Apparently they're going to have a brilliant new winger join their ranks in two months' time."

Magpies had started the season well too, picking up a hard-earned 1-1 draw away to Hulcote United.

It was a solid result.

Charlie's dad had been particularly pleased for Barney.

The point meant the coach would at least have something to build on as he changed teams to make way for the superstar manager taking over at Rovers.

With Peter's injury, it made sense for him start at a club with less pressure – Magpies was the obvious choice.

Joe and Charlie had already discussed the likelihood that their friend wouldn't be lining up alongside them this season.

It was Magpies' gain undoubtedly.

Joe smiled.

"We figured you'd be joining Magpies. That's great, Belly.

"Those doctors have done a great job with your leg. Will you be fit enough to play straight away?"

Peter grimaced at the question, unable to fully hide his frustration.

"No, I'm nowhere near match fit so I was going to ask you guys to help me.

"I can start running and swimming next week and could do with some help. Do you fancy it?"

Joe and Charlie answered without hesitation: "Of course!"

Peter grinned before looking at Charlie again.

"That's great, thanks guys. I'll just have to hope that Fry-inho has a little spare time between all the autographs...."

Charlie began to respond but his reply went unheard.

A bike crashed into the back of Joe, the unexpected impact sent the big lad sprawling to the concrete.

Adam Knight skidded his BMX bike to a halt and laughed at the burly goalkeeper lying on the floor.

"All right ladies? So you're still the golden boy then Fry?

"Don't worry, it won't be long and then you'll be a cripple like your little friend here."

The bully's reckless tackle was still raw with Peter – who had not forgiven the thug for ending his Hall Park trial several months ago

Peter moved forward to grab Adam and yank him off the bike but Charlie pulled him back.

There was no point fighting with him – it was

exactly what the idiot wanted.

As Joe climbed to his feet, Charlie studied the grinning moron leaning on his bike's handlebars a few feet in front of them.

He had no tie, he was wearing trainers and had a freshly shaved head – all things banned under the school's strict rules.

But Adam Knight, as usual, didn't seem to think the rules applied to him.

He was stocky with a fierce glare.

He was not as big as Joe – and had always been wary of the bigger boy throughout primary school – but he towered above Peter and, of course, Charlie.

Charlie saw Joe's hands curl into fists and stretched out a hand on to his forearm to stop him charging straight into the bully.

Satisfied Joe wasn't going to rush at him, Adam turned and saw Lee Brawn biking towards them across the park's large swathe of grass.

Grinning as his friend approached, Adam turned back: "So well done on scoring, Gaspy. Shame you couldn't manage to bag as many as me."

Ignoring the pathetic insult thrown in about his health, Charlie knew exactly what Adam was talking about.

He had scored all four goals as Colts had thrashed Grange Aztec – strongly rumoured to be one of the division's best teams – 4-0 in the opening game.

Adam continued his gloating.

"Even though the Telegraph seems to be in love with you, Fry, if you check the top scorers listing, it's me up at the top, not you."

Lee pulled up alongside Adam.

To the surprise of almost everyone, he had not

been picked up by a team.

The Hall Park trial had not been kind to him.

With the likes of Adam, Charlie and Bishop on the pitch as forwards, he'd been forced to play the key match in midfield – and had been given the run around by both Peter and Charlie.

He had missed the cut, and Lee was still bitter about it.

However he had gone to Choldington Boys' School instead and it meant – to the boys' relief – they barely saw him now.

Lee ran a large hand through his brown hair and wiped the sweat away.

He raised his eyebrows at the two groups facing each other. "Ad, what are you talking to these losers for?"

The sneer in his voice was obvious, the look of disgust written all over his face.

Peter piped up.

"Enjoying the football season, Brawno?"

Joe chuckled as Lee turned pink.

He did not try and hide his anger.

"Get lost, you cripple. I'll break your other leg if you don't shut up."

Adam sniggered again.

"Easy, mate. Let's leave the girls and the superstar to enjoy their celebrity status. I'm sure I'll see them on the pitch soon enough."

Charlie, Peter and Joe watched the bullies ride off towards the park gates, shouting more pointless insults as they went.

Charlie sighed.

"Well, that was pleasant. At least we don't have to put up with those pillocks at training on Wednesday."

Joe nodded.

"We've got Aztec in the next game. I guess we'll find out whether they're any good or whether Knight just got lucky."

Charlie watched the bully and his sidekick disappear on their bikes into the distance.

"Four goals? I think you'd have to get pretty lucky to score that many in a single game."

Joe shrugged.

"Who knows? Still, he's not as good as you, Fry."

At some point in the season, they'd line up against Adam Knight once more.

After what the thug did to Peter in the summer, he knew that Adam's threats could not be taken lightly.

He would be coming after the Boy Wonder this time, Charlie knew, and he had no option but to face him.

11. 'MY WAY IS THE ONLY WAY'

The Hall Park Rovers Under-13s team sat in the centre-circle of the Hall Park pitch as they awaited the arrival of the new manager.

It was a strange atmosphere.

Having spent the summer together the squad knew each other well, meaning there was plenty of jokes and chat whenever they met up.

This time was different.

Tension filled the air as the tight-knit group sat on the field fidgeting and speaking to each other in hushed whispers.

They had a new manager – and, apart from the brief words before the Weavers game, no-one knew exactly what to expect from him.

All of the squad had been sad to see Barney Payne leave them for Magpies.

He had been with them since the summer trials and they had developed a close bond with the veteran coach.

He was kind, he listened to their views and the

training was fun.

And no-one could question his knowledge about soccer because he was a walking encyclopaedia on the game.

Now though Barney was in charge of Magpies and Rovers had a new man at the helm.

Chell Di Santos may have only spoken to the team once – but other changes had already begun creeping in.

Barney had a set routine that he always stuck to.

Play a game on Saturday, train on Sunday.

It was simple but he had insisted on keeping it that way, stressing footballers had to concentrate on schoolwork in the week.

Football, he insisted, was for the weekend.

The set up suited many parents too, who did not want to spend hours on the touchline after a long hard day at work.

But there was a new boss at Rovers now – and a fresh approach too.

The players had been emailed an updated schedule yesterday morning. The weekend sessions would remain the same.

However, there would also be additional training too.

Wednesday nights would be dedicated to 'physical and fitness development' and Friday evenings would be spent covering 'tactics and drills'.

The extra two-hour sessions had raised a few eyebrows among the squad but they knew it was not a request.

It was expected of them.

So the team had turned out as the email demanded – and waited patiently for Rovers' new era to begin.

Exactly at 7pm, Chell Di Santos emerged from the stadium's small tunnel and walked towards the squad.

As usual, he was wearing his long coat and shiny black shoes.

A black hat covered the manager's hair but his stern face was clean shaven, his pointed nose looking even larger underneath the floodlights.

He was flanked by two men: both short middle-aged men wearing brand-new blue tracksuits with the Hall Park badge on the chest.

Di Santos halted a couple of yards short of the waiting squad.

Charlie could not stop staring at the manager's nose, which seemed to be oddly huge in comparison with the rest of his face.

For a second, their eyes met.

Charlie could have sworn that the manager's piercing blue eyes narrowed as they faced at each other.

The boy broke away from the gaze, his heart thumping.

When he looked back at Di Santos, the manager was looking elsewhere.

Had Charlie imagined it?

Chell Di Santos spoke in a clear voice, not particularly loud but firm enough for everyone to hear.

His tone demanded instant respect.

"You have been deemed good enough to play for Hall Park Rovers.

"This should be taken as a great honour because everybody knows that Hall Park is a great club."

He stopped, allowing his words to sink in.

"However ... you have now got to prove

yourselves to me. My standards are higher than anyone else you will ever meet.

"There are three things you need to know about me. Remember them always.

"First I do not tolerate losing.

"Secondly I do not like wimps or people who show-off.

"Third and most importantly, I do not like people who are frightened of hard work."

Charlie could feel Di Santos's glare fall on him again.

He shivered despite the warmth of the mild autumn evening.

The manager continued: "I am a winner.

"And I have the track record to prove it.

"If you listen to me, do as I say and follow instructions, we shall enjoy winning together."

He paused again, allowing the players to absorb his words.

Not one of the footballers moved a muscle or said a word in response.

The silence was unsettling.

When Di Santos spoke again to finish his opening speech, his voice had dropped to barely a whisper.

"Let me repeat this once more because I will not do it again.

"I win.

"I do not lose.

"My way is the only way from now on.

"And if you don't like it or can't cut it under my watch, then you'll never play for Hall Park again."

He looked across the rows of faces looking intently at him.

His gaze settled on Joe, almost challenging the

captain to speak out.

For once Joe stayed quiet.

Satisfied he had got his message across, Di Santos nodded towards the two men before he marched briskly back towards the stadium.

Charlie watched the back of the manager stalk off the field as his mind began to fill with apprehension.

Did he imagine it or had the manager been glaring at him?

Had he done something wrong?

Why did Di Santos give him the creeps so much?

His mind was whirring as Di Santos's two coaches stepped forward to begin the training session.

The taller man spoke first.

"My name is Seth and this is Howard. We are the Rovers' Academy Under-13s coaches now.

"We speak for the Boss on the field.

"We speak, you listen. We tell you what to do and you do it.

"No questions, no funny comments and no smart remarks. No talking unless it's a relevant question.

"Am I making myself clear?"

The squad murmured they understood Seth's words, no-one willing to speak out and bring attention to themselves.

Seth smiled. He seemed pleased there was no answering back from the young footballers.

"Good. Let's get started.

"We'll start off with a nice easy warm-up.

"Ten laps of the pitch as quickly as you can.

"Then the real work begins."

12. SUB

Charlie stared at the Rovers' team sheet, a sinking feeling inside his stomach.

He focused on the sheet of paper pinned to the changing room wall and willed the scribbled note to be wrong.

He was only been named as a substitute for the away game against Aztec.

Crestfallen, the Boy Wonder walked dejectedly to his seat next to Joe and slumped down beside his best friend.

Chell Di Santos had certainly made a statement with his first team selection – he'd benched the club's young superstar without a second thought.

The manager had not even spoken to Charlie about his decision.

As he made clear during his opening speech: it was either his way or you were out.

It had been the one and only time that Di Santos had actually spoken to the team since he had officially taken over the manager's hot-seat.

Since then he had left all instructions to Seth and Howard, who acted like sergeant majors.

Charlie had known there was a problem, even if he could not understand what he had done to be put on the bench.

After his performance in the last game it had never crossed his mind that he would be a substitute against Aztec.

However Charlie was bright enough to realise the new boss was not a fan of his.

What he didn't understand was: why?

Trouble had started to brew when he had been unable to complete the warm-up element on Wednesday evening.

Ten laps were too many for him.

As a result, he had been forced to do train away from the rest of the team.

The issue had not been a lack of effort.

Charlie had given everything to try to complete the warm-up exercise as requested but his lungs just couldn't do it.

And as the session went on, he became tired and had to use his inhaler more and more.

Eventually his father stepped in and told the coaches that Charlie could not cope.

He spent the rest of the evening watching from the sidelines.

Then at the tactics session later in the week, Charlie was put into a small group with Howard taking part in boring shuttle-runs against an automatic timer.

Again, Charlie had to ask to stop way before the others, the lack of oxygen inside his lungs making it impossible for him to continue.

Meanwhile, the first team were being intently coached by Seth over specific free-kicks and corner routines.

Charlie felt like an outsider in his own team.

It may sound silly but he that was how he felt.

And now those nagging insecurities had been proved correct.

He was not the only one hit by Di Santos's changes though.

Joe had been axed as captain – much to everyone's dismay – after Seth told him that Di Santos did not want a goalkeeper to be skipper.

The armband had gone to Seamus, the beefy centre-back who had been part of Adam's gang of bullies during their primary school years.

Since they had become part of the same football team though, things had changed for the better.

At first Charlie and Joe remained cautious around the defender but slowly they had begun to put the past behind them.

Seamus, for his part, now always made an effort to talk – and was no longer acting like a moron towards them.

Joe accepted the shocking decision to change the leadership with good grace, offering the new captain a handshake when he saw the team sheet.

It was awkward but the right thing to do.

Charlie looked at his friend next to him knowing the move had hurt him badly. There was nothing he could say.

After all, it was the manager's decision, not Seamus's.

Joe had barely spoken since they'd arrived in the changing room, not even acknowledging Charlie's demotion to the bench.

And the whole changing room was quiet, unnaturally so.

Grange Aztec played in a state-of-the-art stadium and the room was large, far bigger than their own ancient facilities.

Away changing rooms could be funny places. Despite the modern surroundings, there was no hot water and the drains stank.

Charlie felt sick but he knew the awful stench was not to blame.

Then the manager walked in.

Chell Di Santos looked immaculate in a grey suit, white shirt and blue tie.

Charlie swore that he could see his face in the manager's polished shoes as the boss stopped directly in front of him to give the pre-match team talk.

As he carefully removed his designer shades to ensure his hair remained perfectly in place, Di Santos's piercing eyes scanned the room.

Seth and Howard shuffled behind the boss as the whispered conversations in the room quickly died down.

Within seconds everyone was focused on the manager.

He looked smug as he stood before them.

Di Santos's gaze hovered over a dejected-looking Joe and then moved to Charlie, his mouth forming the slightest hint of a smile.

"This is our first game together," Di Santos's words were deliberately spoken slowly to ensure the boys understood every element.

"My teams win.

"We work hard. We run faster and longer than the

other teams and we win as a result.

"If you do not work hard or you think you are too good to be part of our ethos, then there is no place for you on this team."

There was no mistaking Di Santos's target this time.

Charlie could almost feel the manager's eyes burn through his skull.

What was his problem?

Chell Di Santos put his sunglasses back on and cleared his throat.

"Win. That is what is expected. You are Hall Park's best. Prove it."

Silence hung over the dressing room.

You could hear a pin drop.

The Hall Park Rovers manager swept out of the changing room without another word, happy the squad knew the challenge ahead.

13. AN UNHAPPY WAIT

The bench was not comfortable.

Charlie squirmed on his seat as he watched his teammates struggle against a well-organised Grange Aztec team.

It had not been a happy afternoon for Hall Park so far.

Aztec had decided to defend – and little more.

A heavy defeat can do funny things to a side.

Adam Knight had scored four goals for league leaders Colts against the same Aztec team last week in a 4-0 thrashing.

That drubbing had obviously influenced their manager's thinking for the Hall Park match.

And, as a result, Grange Aztec had put out a team with a single aim: do not lose.

They had one tall striker up front and a midfield playing only metres in front of a back five. It was negative and boring but effective.

The clock was ticking down fast.

Only 10 minutes of the game remained.

Feeling helpless on the sidelines, Charlie fidgeted as the minutes flew by.

Floating uselessly around his vision was the target, the gift that was being wasted for reasons he still could not understand.

Hall Park had enjoyed almost all the possession in the game and had been camped in the Aztec half but could not find that elusive goal.

Bishop had hit the woodwork three times and Johnny Somore – who had taken Charlie's place in the starting line-up – had seen a goal disallowed for a foul only the linesman saw.

Chances had come and gone yet the score remained 0-0.

The Hall Park supporters became unhappier as frustrations grew; calls for Charlie became louder with every chance the team missed.

This was a surprise to no-one.

When the teams ran out for kick-off, there had been gasps of shock as fans realised the Boy Wonder would not be not be starting.

Charlie could hear the whispers as he went through the warm-up with the rest of the squad before kick-off.

"Is he injured?"

"Well, he's fit enough to be a sub, isn't he?"

"I hear a Premier League club have signed him and he's off tomorrow."

"Does he have breathing problems?"

"He looks fine to me, Trev."

"It's all the speculation. It's gone to his head. He even calls himself Boy Wonder these days and he doesn't even answer to Charlie."

"He's looking a little thin."

"Should we take him out for a burger some time and get some meat on those ribs?"

"Can we win without him?"

They were only some of the comments Charlie overheard as he warmed up, a bizarre mixture of the absurd, fantasy and sheer nonsense.

There were plenty more that he didn't hear – and the fussy crowd was becoming unhappier as the minutes ticked by.

All of Hall Park Rover's subs had been warming up along the touchline for the most of the second half.

None of them had been used yet though.

Charlie had been with them but a large crowd of supporters had gathered around to ask why the Boy Wonder wasn't playing.

Eventually Seth had ushered Charlie back to the bench, and told him to remain there until called upon.

There was now only eight minutes of the game remaining.

For the first time though Charlie wasn't actually watching the game – he was keeping a close eye on Chell Di Santos instead.

The manager stood like a statue for the opening half, not moving a muscle even as the crowd became more anxious.

It had taken Johnny's disallowed goal to finally break the iceman's image.

As the flag went up to rule out the goal, there was a flash of temper that had not yet been seen by the Hall Park team or fans.

He raced up to the linesman jabbing his bony finger into match official's chest.

With a look of horror on his face, the match

official – a kindly man with white hair and aged in his 60s – shrank away from a furious Di Santos.

Seth grabbed his furious boss and guided him back to the dugout and away from the confrontation with the assistant ref.

Back in the dugout the Hall Park manager was still furious.

Within seconds he had leapt out again and began to roar at Hall Park's full-backs, insisting they push up the pitch.

Next he waved at Joe to order him stand outside his penalty area and double up as a sweeper to keep the pressure on the home team.

It was the first time Charlie had ever seen Chell Di Santos lose his cool.

And it wasn't pretty.

The man was cold, calculating and had a short fuse too.

Not a good combination, Charlie thought to himself, as he finally turned his attention back to the game.

A corner provided Hall Park with yet another chance to score the goal that would win the game.

The ball swung into the penalty area and met firmly by the head of Seamus, making a rare trip forward from his usual defensive position.

With the Aztec goalkeeper stranded, the header grazed the top of the bar and flew over for a goal kick.

Di Santos threw his arms up in frustration again, speaking loudly in a foreign language that Charlie did not understand.

Whether you understood Italian or not, it was clear the new Hall Park manager was deeply unhappy.

Once his rant had ended, the manager turned to Charlie – his voice back to its usual icy tone.

"Boy. Get ready. You're coming on."

14. LAST GASP

Charlie did not need to be asked twice.

He had his tracksuit top off and he was eagerly bouncing up and down on the touchline within seconds.

Seth waved to the ref to indicate Hall Park wanted to make a substitution.

Thirty seconds later, the ball bounced out of play and change could be made.

The Boy Wonder estimated he had two minutes of normal time plus any added injury time to make the difference.

All he needed was the ball.

He clenched his teeth with determination.

He could do this.

Charlie looked expectantly at the manager standing a few metres to his right.

Barney had always given them instructions when they were coming on as a sub; what position they would be playing in, perhaps the role they needed to fill and anything he thought may give the team a small advantage.

But Chell Di Santos looked straight ahead, not giving Charlie a second glance.

Johnny scampered over the touchline, aware of the need not to take up any more time.

The strikers shook hands and Charlie stepped on to the pitch at last.

The crowd burst into life, excited that the Boy Wonder was finally set to make a belated entrance to the game.

Blocking out the din from the stands Charlie stared back at his manager in the hope of the merest hint of guidance or encouragement.

Nothing was forthcoming.

Di Santos did even show a flicker of recognition as he glared in completely the opposite direction to Charlie.

The vein in the manager's thin scrawny neck was pulsing with anger, looking like it may pop at any second.

The thought made Charlie snigger, although he did not know why.

He trotted out towards Bishop, who was standing red-faced with his hands on hips.

The burly striker didn't mince his words.

"About time he put you on, Fry! Where are you playing? Up top with me?"

Charlie shrugged his shoulders and shook his head, confused.

"No idea. I guess so. He didn't say."

Bishop raised his eyebrows in surprise, wiping the sweaty hair away from his forehead as he did so.

"This bloke is a complete joke."

The game started again and meant Charlie didn't

get the opportunity to respond.

Bishop's words warmed him though – perhaps he and Joe were not alone in disliking the new manager after all.

The Boy Wonder glanced at the scoreboard with the ball being booted deep into Hall Park's half as an exhausted Aztec team looked to run the clock down.

He now had only 90 seconds plus injury time.

Score a goal.

Win the match.

Prove the manager he deserved to be in this team.

Charlie began jogging towards his own half looking to get involved straight away.

He knew he might not even touch the ball before the ref blew the whistle for full time.

He had to try though.

Seamus won the ball back for Hall Park and sent a long hopeful punt forward with a big clump of his right boot.

Standing in the centre circle, the ball went high over Charlie's head.

"BOY!"

Chell Di Santos screamed at the top of his voice as he waved his arms in circles.

"UP! UP! UP!"

It took Charlie a moment to realise the manager was talking to him.

"NOW!!!"

Charlie began sprinting as fast as he could towards the penalty area.

Behind him, the manager was still shouting but Charlie no longer heard him.

He was watching the ball as Bishop wrestled with Aztecs' two strapping centre-backs on the left wing.

Somehow the Hall Park target man managed to slip the pair, swivelled and floated the ball towards the penalty spot.

The Aztec keeper moved forward to catch the ball but hesitated and stepped back towards his goal unwilling to commit.

As he arrived on the edge of the penalty box, Charlie instinctively knew what was going to happen.

Rovers' right winger Shivander Silvio challenged the small left-back for the header, the ball dropped past them both and ran free across the six-yard box.

Charlie read the situation, ghosting into the large space behind the pair with barely a second thought.

The ball was moving away from the goal when he reached it and an Aztec defender was racing across the goal to intercept the potential danger.

In a split second, Charlie realised this was the only chance he would get.

But he was not facing the goal so he couldn't use the target.

Also the defender was between him and the net.

Even if he could somehow position the target on the goal, the ball would surely cannon straight into the defender's stomach.

He had no choice.

For once his magic gift could not help him.

Charlie reached the ball a fraction before the Aztec player.

He knew what to do.

He wrapped his right foot around the ball and tried to carefully dink it back over the head of the onrushing player.

The scampering Aztec defender was too close though.

The ball flicked his chest and looped towards the goal with almost all the pace removed by the deflection.

The goalkeeper was completely wronged-footed by the deflection and watched, helplessly rooted to the spot.

Charlie felt like time stood still as the ball slowly spun towards the goal ... but agonisingly drifted past the post.

Unable to halt his momentum and his attention focused completely on the ball, the beefy Aztec defender barged straight into Charlie.

His bulky shoulder sent the Boy Wonder spinning to the floor and knocked the few remaining dregs of air out of him.

Charlie fell down and did not get up.

Part of the crowd began to celebrate, mistakenly believing Charlie had bagged a last-gasp winner.

But they were wrong.

The game was still goalless.

Exhausted from the sprint, Charlie could feel his lungs begging for air, sparking his usual cough as he tried to calm his breathing.

As the striker choked on his hands and knees, the Aztec players surrounded the referee arguing with the official.

The ref, a dark-haired man with his black shorts pulled up to his belly button, had correctly awarded a corner, a decision that had outraged the entire home team.

Everyone had seen the ball deflect off the Aztec player.

But Charlie suspected the home team was trying to waste time, putting extra pressure on the ref to end the game.

It was a cheap trick.

He dragged himself to his feet, ignoring the fuss around him.

By now they were deep into injury time with perhaps only a minute left.

It was now or never.

Charlie stumbled to the edge of the penalty area, little more than a spectator once more.

He was doubled-over trying to catch his breath with Aztec players continuing to grumble around him as they prepared to defend the game's final attack.

Seconds later the ball was whipped in by Silvio with Seamus once again causing mayhem in the opposition's penalty area.

The Hall Park captain's towering header crashed straight into the defender who was jumping alongside him.

The ball dropped and bounced tantalisingly inside the Aztecs' six-yard box.

Everyone seemed to stop and stare at the loose ball as the ref moved his whistle to his lips to bring the game to a close.

Then a boot swung from nowhere and crashed the ball past the onrushing goalkeeper and into the roof of the net.

GOAL!

Bishop had bagged the winner with lightning quick reactions to pounce on the ball first before anyone else reacted.

He had done it.

Bishop was already rushing towards the corner of the pitch in wild celebration as the ref blew the final whistle to bring the game to an end.

They had done it – just.

Still out of breath, Charlie stood alone as the exhausted Aztec players sunk to their knees in despair around him.

His jubilant teammates mobbed the goal-scorer in front of the ecstatic Hall Park fans but Charlie did not join them. He needed his inhaler – and quickly.

Hall Park had nicked it with the very last kick of the match.

Chell Di Santos's reign as Rovers' Under-13s boss had got off to a winning start.

15. THE WARNING

A mixture of jubilant and excited chatter filled the away dressing room as the Hall Park Under-13s squad celebrated Bishop's late winner.

The relief was obvious.

It had been close but they'd done it.

They'd found a way to win, never giving up until the final kick.

Barney would be so proud when he heard.

The negative Aztec game plan had been shattered with Bishop's final swing of the boot – attack had won the day over defence.

It felt good.

After being winded so badly, Charlie had avoided the traditional post-match handshakes and returned to the dressing room seeking his inhaler.

His breathing was now under control but he could feel the soreness across his body where the big defender had charged into him.

It would hurt like hell tomorrow, Charlie was sure of it.

Seth and Howard walked into the room, whispering to each other.

They did not make eye contact with anyone but stood near the squad's tactics board with serious faces.

There were no smiles on the faces of the coaches, unlike everyone else in the room.

Joe stood and piped up above the din: "Hey Seth, do you know any of the other results?"

Seth looked up at the young goalkeeper, who barely had a speck of dirt on him, revealing precisely how unadventurous the Aztec team had been.

He blew out his cheeks but replied: "I know a few."

The room quietened down almost instantly as the lads turned to hear how their rivals had done.

"Thrapborough Colts beat Collingworth Wrenn 8-0."

Charlie's heart sank.

Adam Knight would be gloating again on Monday. He wondered how many goals the bully had bagged this time.

Seth continued, aware the whole team was hanging on his every word.

"Weavers scored a late goal to draw away at Hulcote United."

Hulcote would be Rovers' next opponents on Wednesday evening – the team's first night game under the Hall Park floodlights.

"And Magpies?" Joe asked.

Seth shifted: "They were beaten 5-0 away by Wootton Pools.

"They were a man short for the last 30 minutes – due to another injury."

Smiles that had been so wide moments ago faltered.

The Magpies side was made up of their friends, good players they'd spent the summer with.

No-one wanted to see them lose.

And that was a big defeat.

"Now you know," Seth continued. "Right you lot, it's time to hit the showers."

"Wait."

Charlie knew Di Santos's voice without even needing to look in the direction of the dressing room door.

A pin drop could have been heard as the manager walked towards the tactics board without another word.

The manager reached up and carefully unpinned the team sheet before turning to face the squad.

He did not speak until he was certain he had the squad's full attention.

When he was happy no-one was distracted, Di Santos tore the team sheet in two and let the paper drop to the floor.

Charlie looked at Joe and raised his eyebrows in surprise.

When the manager spoke, his voice had dropped to barely a whisper.

"Today was a disgrace.

"I am ashamed to call you 'my team'. It will never happen again."

His piercing blue eyes swept the changing room, deliberately searching for any challenge to his authority.

It was Bishop who spoke up: "But we won?"

Di Santos's thin lips turned into a cruel grin.

"Obviously you're happy to settle for second best, Brian? Perhaps 15 laps of the pitch will keep you quiet in future?"

Bishop stood, his face turning purple.

Charlie could see his anger rising and felt sorry for his buddy.

He had scored the winner, bust a gut for the team and played a great game – and was being punished for it?

It didn't seem right.

"Are you kidding?" Bishop asked angrily.

"I never kid," snapped Di Santos. "Let's make it 20 laps, shall we?"

Bishop glared at him. "What?"

"Fine. 25 laps, it is. Off you go."

Red-faced with fury, Bishop stormed out of dressing room towards the pitch for the unexpected extra workout.

Howard followed the striker out without a word, the coach obviously used to this type of punishment for players who argued with the boss.

When the door closed shut, Di Santos spoke again.

"Now, does anyone else fancy an extra workout?"

No one uttered a word.

"Good. You need to be fitter, smarter and listen to our tactics. Today was a shambles, an absolute embarrassment to me, your parents and the fans.

"We almost made Hall Park a laughing stock. I will not tolerate this.

"We'll start with fitness this week. Be ready."

Di Santos spoke with such venom that little drops of spit flew from his mouth as the words came out.

The boss marched to the door but hesitated as he reached for the door handle, almost as if he had remembered something else.

"Oh, there is one final thing.

"If I see any of my players refusing to shake hands with the opposition after a match again, you will never play for Hall Park again."

The manager turned and left, the threat hanging over the shocked squad.

16. FIGHTING TO BE FIT

With Di Santos's words ringing in his ears, Charlie spent the rest of the afternoon working on his fitness.

Apart from the constant ache in his ribs after being barged into, he had plenty of energy left to burn off.

Playing for six minutes had not been too draining.

And at least he had a helper to keep him company.

Harry Fry eagerly timed his big brother's shuttle runs in their back garden before holding down Charlie's ankles for a sit-up session.

The six-year-old was football-mad and never stopped trying to give Charlie advice on how to be a better player.

The little lad – who had short spiky blonde hair and a big gappy smile as he waited for his adult teeth to arrive – was a pain in the neck for Charlie much of the time.

Harry often charged around the Fry house with his space station toys, thudding into furniture during wild rocket adventure games.

But he idolised his brother, and wanted to spend every moment with him. And, as much as he annoyed Charlie, he was good fun too.

It was the first time after a Rovers match the Boy Wonder had not been glued to his tablet waiting for the Telegraph's match report to go live.

He had barely featured in the game and the match had been truly boring, meaning Charlie's usual enthusiasm was dampened.

As the pair worked out, Charlie replayed Di Santos's words over and over in his mind.

Harry was chattering merrily about the game but Charlie's thoughts were miles away, questions swimming through his mind.

Why was the manager so unhappy after a win?

Bishop had barely said a word to him. Why had he been treated so unfairly?

Was Di Santos talking about Charlie's fitness or the entire team's?

And did Di Santos even know why he could not run as far as the others?

The handshake comment had been obviously aimed at Charlie – but he had been rushing off to try to find his inhaler.

He wasn't rude and was never a bad sport. He had been struggling to breathe. Why couldn't Di Santos see that?

Their mum Molly interrupted Charlie's train of thought as he was busy completing his third lap of the garden.

"Dinner, you two!"

"Thanks, Mum!"

Charlie answered for both of them, Harry already moving towards the kitchen.

Charlie watched his brother race up the back garden steps into the house. Harry did not have cystic fibrosis and ate a huge amount for such a skinny boy.

Charlie envied Harry, often wondering what hunger felt like.

His own appetite was fairly impressive for someone with CF – but he still struggled to put on any weight.

And when he was feeling ill, weight dropped off him in the blink of an eye.

Charlie shrugged and headed towards the kitchen, determined to try to eat at least some of his mum's cooking.

If he was going to be fitter and stronger as the new Rovers manager demanded, then he needed to eat plenty.

By the time Charlie had removed his trainers and washed his hands, Harry was already tucking into his fish fingers, chips and beans.

Charlie slid into the seat next to his brother, who – between mouthfuls – was busy telling their mum about the garden training.

Charlie looked at his plate and took a deep breath.

"I have to eat," he reminded himself as he picked up the fork and speared a couple of chips before slowly putting them into his mouth.

Trying to take his mind off the food that he didn't really want to eat, Charlie glanced up as his dad Liam – a burly man with huge hands and a bald head – walked into the room.

He did not sit down even though his dinner was waiting on the table too.

Suddenly he realised both of his parents were anxiously looking at him, with worried expressions upon their faces.

He knew instantly something was wrong.

Charlie's stomach lurched.

"What?"

His voice came out with a boom, far louder than he had planned.

Harry stopped chattering and looked at his brother, surprised by the interruption.

Mystified, the younger boy then looked up at his parents too.

Molly shifted in her seat, twisting a strand of her long brown hair nervously around her fingers.

"Tell him."

Charlie's gut turned again; his mum's voice sounded so serious.

He stood up, forgetting about the meal that he had never wanted to eat, and turned towards his father.

Liam Fry was a builder, a man of few words and huge muscles.

He did not speak often but, when he did, people listened.

"Tell me what, Dad?"

Liam stroked the stubble on his chin thoughtfully before replying.

When he spoke, his words were gentle and carefully chosen.

"Son, there's an article on the paper's website. It is...."

Charlie interrupted.

"The match report? I know, Dad, I read that every week! If that's…"

The Boy Wonder stopped mid-sentence as his father raised a shovel-sized palm to silence him.

"Charlie. Let me finish.

"The newspaper reporter interviewed Chell Di Santos after the game. They talked to him…"

Charlie's dad paused as he struggled to find the right words.

"…about you."

17. THE INTERVIEW

Everyone stopped. Even Harry was no longer eating.

Charlie could feel his eyes brim with tears.

"What did he say, Dad?" His voice was a whisper.

Mr Fry looked sternly at his boy.

"Don't you worry about it, Son. I'll sort this out."

"NO! I want to see it now!"

Charlie shouted the sentence at his parents, and began to move away from the table to check his tablet.

What had Di Santos said about him?

Liam stepped across the doorway, blocking his son's route.

"No, Son. Back to the dinner table please.

"I've rung Mr Di Santos and left a message. We'll get to the bottom of this soon enough."

Charlie looked at his dad, a warm feeling of gratitude rushing over him.

Whenever he was in trouble, tired or feeling unwell, his mum and dad were always there to help him out.

They were the best.

But this was something different. He was in secondary school now – he was no longer a little child at primary school.

He had to know what had been said about him.

"Thanks Dad. I need to see that article though."

Unseen by Charlie, his mum had moved to stand right behind him and placed her hand gently on his bony shoulder.

"Charlie's right, Liam. He should read the article.

"He's getting older now and needs to understand that people have different opinions and thoughts – no matter how wrong or hurtful they are. We can't protect him forever."

Charlie turned and gave his mum a hug.

Her purple top was soon wet with his tears.

Charlie did not know why he was crying – he had not even read the stupid article yet – but he could not stop as his mum held him close.

His dad spoke again: "Fair enough. Let's eat dinner and we'll look at the article together."

"And me?"

Harry's small voice piped up from the table.

"Not a chance, young man! It's bath-time for you after dinner!" laughed Molly, who eased Charlie away from her and back towards his seat.

Despite managing to stop the tears, Charlie could not find the stomach to eat any more food.

He pushed the chips around his plate and hoped his parents wouldn't tell him off.

His body desperately needed the calories – but he couldn't face eating today.

He needed to read that article.

To upset his dad took something special.

Finally the meal was over.

Harry, tomato sauce plastered around his mouth, was busy tucking into a bowl of strawberry ice-cream when Charlie was eventually given permission to leave the table.

He did not waste any time as he raced into the living room and snatched his tablet up from the couch.

Charlie could feel his leg bounce up and down as he waited for the Telegraph website to appear on the screen.

His dad came and sat on the sofa next to him as the page loaded.

It did not take long.

"Remember, Son, I'm going to sort all this nonsense out."

Charlie instinctively opened the sports pages and clicked into the section called "Hall Park Rovers".

He gasped as he saw the site's main headline.

"Boy Wonder 'too unfit' to play for Hall Park"
By Andrew Hallmaker

Charlie felt his dad grip his arm as he clicked on the headline.

He crossed his fingers, hoping the paper had just created a sensational headline as he began reading.

Hall Park Rovers manger Chell Di Santos today defended his decision to bench Charlie Fry and insisted: "He's not fit enough."

The shock decision to name the Boy Wonder among the substitutes nearly cost Rovers' Under-13s dearly as they scraped a narrow 1-0 win over Grange Aztec.

A Brian Bishop goal deep into injury time settled the game, which saw Rovers stay in second place behind the impressive Thrapborough Colts.

However, it was Di Santos's surprise decision to axe his star striker that was the game's main talking point.

Speaking after the game, the Hall Park Under-13s boss was adamant that Fry needed to raise his fitness levels – and soon.

Charlie could barely believe what he was reading.

Di Santos had barely bothered to speak to him since he had become manager – and yet he didn't mind telling the local newspaper?

It was not fair.

His dad's phone vibrated and they looked at each other.

His dad stood up, looked at the screen to see who was calling, and said: "I'll take this in the kitchen, Son.

"You stay in here."

Something in his dad's tone made Charlie follow the order.

He knew it was the manager and he was desperate to hear the conversation.

But his dad was not someone to disobey, especially the mood he was in at the moment.

The kitchen door closed shut so Charlie turned his attention back to the article.

He said: "Charlie Fry is a player who can score goals.

"But he needs to work harder, much harder. His fitness is an absolute disgrace.

"I will not have a player in my team who can't – or maybe won't – run for the team.

"This is about attitude. Charlie Fry must do better in every department.

"If his attitude and dedication doesn't improve considerably in the coming weeks, then he is finished at Hall Park."

The rest of the article concentrated on the game with Bishop's goalscoring heroics only getting a tiny mention in the last sentence of the article.

Charlie scratched his head, lost in thought.

He had no future at Hall Park unless he improved his fitness?

What?

And how much fitter could he get in three days before their next game?

Charlie knew he was never going to be able to run as far as the others.

His lungs simply did not allow it and that's why he had to select when to run and when to take a breather.

Barney had understood.

Why couldn't Di Santos?

Something funny was going on here and it made Charlie uncomfortable.

As he closed the tablet's screen, he could hear his dad's voice getting louder in the kitchen.

Charlie's ears pricked up.

"Look here, I don't care who you think you are.

"My son always gives his best, and your attitude disgusts me.

"He is a great football player.

"Everyone can see that but you, apparently.

"You know exactly what condition he has and how that affects him.

"Blabbing your big mouth off to the paper is

hardly helpful, is it?"

Charlie felt a rush of gratitude shoot through his body.

His mum and dad always supported him, whether it was training in the freezing cold or by his hospital bedside when his lungs had an infection.

His eyes filled with tears again as he thought about the pair of them – strict and fussy, they were still the best.

A booming voice from the kitchen stopped his thoughts in their tracks.

"NEVER SAY THAT TO ME – OR ANYONE ELSE – AGAIN!

"YOU ARE A SPINELESS, PATHETIC LITTLE MAN. THIS CONVERSATION IS OVER!"

Red-faced with anger, Liam stormed into the sitting room and towered above Charlie, who had never seen his dad so upset.

But when he spoke, his voice was calm.

"Son, you'll get no more problems from that man.

"If you do, you come and see me."

18. COMEBACK

Charlie stood in front of the team sheet for the Hulcote match, barely believing his eyes.

Somehow he was back in the Hall Park Rovers starting line-up.

Despite Di Santos's complaints.

Despite the threats being made in the Telegraph.

Despite his dad shouting at the manager and hanging up the phone on him.

The manager had not spoken to Charlie since but it appeared he was ready to forgive and forget.

Charlie sniffed and wiped his nose with the back of his hand, unable to take his eyes off the team sheet.

Something was strange though.

His name – which usually appeared near the bottom of the starting line-up among the strikers with Bishop – was fifth in the line-up.

It didn't seem right.

Charlie shrugged, putting it out of his mind.

He was playing again and that was the main thing.

Perhaps his dad's rant had done the trick.

Who knew when it came to Di Santos?

The Boy Wonder had arrived early as usual with Joe and the changing room was still half-empty, although was rapidly filling up.

He plonked himself down in his usual seat next to Joe, who was pulling on his fresh goalkeeper jersey, and began rooting around in his kitbag for a tissue.

Charlie had started a cold the night before.

At the moment it did not seem too serious but even a head cold could easily put him in hospital.

Knowing his mum would stop him playing, he had hid the fact that he felt unwell from his parents all day.

He had even forced himself to eat dinner to try to keep them from twigging his secret.

But he was getting worse and he wouldn't be able to hide it much longer.

His nose was running almost all the time and he felt shivery despite the warm autumn evening.

Charlie knew he had to play well against Hulcote.

Di Santos was prepared to give him a chance – and he couldn't waste it.

He could do it.

All he needed was this chance, one opportunity to show the manager he could score goals – and would bust a gut for the team.

A stupid cold wouldn't stop him.

He looked at Joe, who was watching him with a stern look on his face.

"Charlie, you're not well enough to play. You need to tell the coaches. This is stupid."

Joe was being a good friend, concerned about his mate's health. But for some reason, his words of caution annoyed Charlie.

He snapped: "Shut up, Joe. I'm fine. It's just a little cold."

He sniffed again.

Joe did not drop the concerned look: "Charlie...."

Charlie stood up: "No, Joe, I'm not talking about it anymore. I'm playing today."

Joe bit his lip, aware his friend's mind was made up.

By now the dressing room was almost full.

It was 40 minutes until kick-off and excitement was growing as the players prepared for their first evening kick-off.

Lost amid the chatter of the room, no-one else had overheard Charlie and Joe's discussion or even noticed as the best friends pulled their kits without the usual banter.

Five minutes later, Seth and Howard arrived followed a few seconds later by the manager, who had, for once, ditched his sunglasses.

His gaze fell on Charlie but as usual moved away instantly without a flicker of recognition.

Charlie blew out his cheeks.

Di Santos had obviously not learned any manners since his little chat with Charlie's dad.

The sudden arrival of the boss and the coaches sent the room into silence.

As usual, Di Santos stood in the middle of the room, surveying the scene and waiting for complete quiet before speaking.

When he spoke, he barked out the words and eagerly scanned the room looking for anyone who may want to disagree with him.

"Gentlemen, things are going to be a little different today.

"First, after the disaster against Aztec, I've changed formation.

"We are playing 3-5-2 today with wingbacks. These roles will be filled on the right by Paulo ... and on the left by Charlie.

"Seamus, you play as sweeper. Everyone else should know their position."

Charlie gulped.

Left wing back?

That a role involving an awful lot of running and was one of the most demanding positions in football.

Besides, he had never played in that position before.

"Secondly, we are having a longer pre-match warm-up today.

"This is our only team talk. After this, we will go out on to the pitch, go through an in-depth warm-up and move straight into the game.

"Last weekend you started off the match far too sleepily. It will not happen again with this fresh approach."

Chell Di Santos stood with his arms crossed, almost daring someone to be brave enough to speak against his wishes.

Charlie watched him eyeball Bishop – who moments earlier had been grumbling about the extra laps of the pitch he'd been forced to run after the last game.

The striker though lowered his eyes to the ground, unwilling to risk yet another argument with the mean boss.

Satisfied they all understood, Chell Di Santos smiled.

It was an unpleasant grin, his thin lips turning the

expression into a sneer.

His pointed fingers brushed casually through his hair as he moved towards the dressing room door.

"Good. Remember Hall Park, I expect only two things from my teams.

"One. Everyone must give 100 per cent effort when they are out on the pitch – whether it is training, in the warm-up or in a match.

"No exceptions.

"Two. My teams always win.

"We play to win and defeat is not an option. Never forget either of these things."

The manager did not wait for the reaction this time. He twisted around, his long overcoat flowing out like a cape behind him as he did so.

Charlie felt Joe give him a supportive pat on the back.

He nodded his thanks but his heart was beating fast.

Yes, he was playing against Hulcote but in an unusual position with an extra-long warm-up to endure.

And his head cold seemed to be getting worse.

Charlie was unsure if it was the shivers or nerves that were making him feel so ill.

He'd soon find out.

19. A PAINFUL WARM-UP

Joe stretched out on his back as the warm-up finally came to an end in the centre of the Hall Park pitch.

It had been gruelling.

The goalkeeper propped himself up on to his elbows and looked back to see Charlie.

His best friend had done brilliantly – far better than Joe had first feared – but still trailed the others by a long way.

Joe scowled at the coaches, who were watching his friend intently.

Seth and Howard had spent more than half an hour warming up the team – and most of the activities had been shattering.

But the last task had been on a different level.

The players, even the substitutes, had been ordered to climb the main stand's stairs 10 times as quickly as they could.

It was bizarre.

As the crowd filled the stadium before the game,

the Under-13s were forced to dodge around them as they tried to find their seats.

Joe had spent most of the exercise running behind Charlie – taking up the last position in the entire squad.

He could not understand the thinking of the manager.

At this rate they would be exhausted even before the kick-off.

It made no sense.

Nose streaming and his skin as white as a ghost, Charlie had somehow managed to complete the running but the stadium steps challenge was too much.

Halfway through Charlie had been forced to stop, unable to keep up.

Joe halted with his friend for a few moments only for Howard to shout angrily at him to keep moving.

Reluctantly Joe obeyed, continued the climb and left Charlie alone.

He could see the coaches making notes as he ran up and down the ancient stairs of the stadium.

Joe was relieved when he spotted his friend running again but knew Charlie was by now a long way behind his teammates.

A couple of others had stopped too – even Seamus had been forced to take a quick breather – but none for anywhere near as long as the Boy Wonder.

Charlie finally finished the exercise and crashed on to the floor next to Joe, wheezing as he tried to regain his breath.

He sounded terrible.

As Joe looked at his exhausted friend, his eyes

caught sight of their manager sitting alone high up in the stands.

He was staring directly at them – and he looked mad.

Shocked by the thunderous look on Di Santos's face, Joe dragged a confused Charlie to his feet and told him to begin to stretch.

"What ... are ... you ... doing?"

Charlie's words came out slowly as he tried to get enough air to stop the world spinning.

Joe whispered a reply, barely moving his lips.

"Trust me, Fry. He's watching us."

Charlie didn't need to ask who Joe was talking about.

He began to scan the crowd for the demon football manager who was so intent on making his life a misery.

Joe continued: "We need to show that idiot that we are not tired. We're ready for the game, no matter what he throws at us."

Charlie stayed silent but he knew Joe was, as usual, looking out for him.

He still felt dizzy as he tried to follow Joe's stretches.

But slowly he began to feel normal again as the Hulcote team ran out to start the game.

The away team – wearing a horrid orange jersey with green shorts and socks – had enjoyed a gentle warm-up for 15 minutes before spending the next ten minutes in the dressing room having a final team talk.

It was the same approach Hall Park had taken in the short spell when Barney had been their manager.

But it was different now.

In complete contrast to their opponents, Hall

Park's players walked slowly on to the pitch feeling their leg muscles ache and throb.

And the game had not even kicked off yet.

That was not the only problem either.

Di Santos had switched the team's formation overnight and barely a word had been said about it.

What kind of manager did that?

Charlie knew he was playing left wing back … and that was pretty much it.

As the Hall Park players dragged themselves towards the home end, Charlie couldn't escape a simple fact.

He had a very bad feeling about all this.

20. DISASTER

The Hall Park stadium announcer could hardly hide the glee in his voice as he introduced the teams.

"Ladies and gentlemen, thank you for helping make tonight's game a landmark evening – this is the biggest crowd for a Hall Park Academy match ever!

"There is a whopping 362 of you inside the ground tonight.

"Let's hope the game – and our great young team – can live up to expectations."

The name of each Hall Park Rovers player was greeted with loud cheers by the home crowd but no-one got a reception like Charlie.

He remained a hero in the fans' eyes, no matter what problems he had with the new boss.

He blushed as he saw a new banner being unfolded at the far end of the pitch.

It said:

"We Believe In You, Boy Wonder."

The Rovers' blue shirts gathered in a team huddle with seconds to go before the pre-match coin toss.

As blunt as ever, Seamus was straight to the point.

"We've got to win tonight, boys. Get into them straight away.

"Press, press, press. And let's send a message to the rest of the league.

"We've got this, Rovers."

The rest of the team grunted their agreement and broke away from the huddle, moving to different parts of the pitch.

Charlie jogged to the left wing. He checked over his shoulder to see Joe jump up and touch the crossbar with ease.

Joe's mum Steffi stood only a couple of metres away from Charlie on the touchline.

She raised her eyebrows and whispered: "Charlie Fry, what on earth are you doing? You're in the wrong position!"

Steffi was great fun, a loud character that could not sit still.

Both of Joe's parents were quite formidable – it was easy to see where he got his considerable size from.

Mrs Foster had known Charlie and his family since he was a toddler and she was like a second mum to him.

She knew the trouble he was having with Di Santos – but did not let this show as she spoke.

As Seamus correctly called the coin toss and opted to kick off the match, Charlie quietly replied: "What?"

Steffi stepped closer, leaning over the ancient wooden advertising hoarding to get closer.

"You're our best striker, Mr Boy Wonder. You're

in the wrong position, you nitwit!"

Charlie shrugged.

"Not today. I'm playing wing back."

For once Mrs Foster seemed lost for words.

She stepped back from the touchline muttering in a low voice.

Charlie could only make out a few words.

"What an idiot he is."

Despite feeling awful Charlie couldn't help but smirk.

Steffi was one of the most loyal people you could ever meet, and he knew exactly who the comment was aimed at.

He turned around to try to focus on the opposition: Hulcote United.

Unlike the first game of the season against Weavers, where Hall Park had faced a team of giants, Hulcote were completely different.

Most of their team were only Charlie's size – many of their players were far, far smaller than the other sides they'd faced this season.

Relief flooded through him.

He was dreading facing a huge striker and being embarrassed defensively like Bishop managed in last year's school final.

It was an unpleasant memory, one he didn't want to repeat.

Charlie could see the two lads lining up against him on Hulcote's right flank.

Both were small and skinny with big smiles on their faces as they whispered together.

Charlie knew one of them vaguely – he was sure the blonde winger, Ben, went to his school although they'd never really had the chance to speak.

Ben nodded a quick hello towards Charlie as the referee blew the whistle to start the match.

The Boy Wonder returned Ben's greeting as Bishop and Johnny kicked off the game that Hall Park – and Charlie – had to win.

His relief did not last long.

Hulcote may have been small but Charlie had misjudged them – their attackers were lightning quick and very direct.

The first 30 seconds showed they would be no pushovers.

A long ball was pinged straight over Charlie's head into the large space behind him.

Sensing an opportunity to get behind the unorganised Hall Park defence, Ben glided past Charlie as if the Boy Wonder's feet were stuck in treacle.

The flying winger pinched the ball as Charlie desperately tried to slide and put it out of play. Moving at top speed, Ben vaulted the tackle and was away.

Seamus galloped over to cover but was caught off-balance as the Hulcote player flicked the ball one side of him and ran around the other.

Seth was screaming in Charlie's direction but he did not listen – he was watching aghast at the awful start they'd made.

Ben was through one-on-one with Joe with less than a minute gone.

Joe came off his line in a flash.

He plunged straight down towards Ben's feet and clawed the ball into his stomach just as the forward prepared to pull the trigger.

Cries for a penalty went up from the Hulcote

players, bench and supporters, but the referee waved the appeals away.

It had been a fair tackle, a superb piece of goalkeeping.

Joe didn't stop there either.

The Boy Wonder got up off the floor and immediately saw what Joe wanted to do.

Charlie spread his arms wide to show he was ready for the ball and sensed the opportunity for an immediate counter-attack.

In a move they'd practiced thousands of times on The Rec, Joe's long throw was perfect – landing a few feet ahead of Charlie.

It allowed him to gallop into the space that Ben had left behind him.

Hulcote's right-back did not want to make a tackle high up the pitch and retreated back towards his own goal.

His reluctance to tackle gave Charlie plenty of time to pick out a pass.

It was a mistake.

The floating target inside Charlie's eyesight – which had been barely used in the past couple of weeks – sprang to life again.

As he passed over the half-way line, the Boy Wonder saw Bishop begin to move.

In the blink of an eye, he placed the target directly between Hulcote's two centre-backs.

It flashed green and Charlie kicked with all his might.

Curling in the air, the through-ball went straight between the surprised defenders and put Bishop through on goal.

The crowd held its breath as Bishop took it in his

stride and ... completely missed his kick. The ball trickled out for goal-kick.

Bishop angrily looked down at the pitch, and suggested the ball had bobbled at the exact moment he'd tried to shoot.

Straight away Hulcote got the game moving again, once more mounting an attack down Charlie's side.

The pace of the game was intense.

The right-back had the ball with Ben in front of him.

Charlie looked round, saw little cover behind him so dropped off and waited for more help to arrive.

"FRY!"

There was no mistaking the voice.

Chell Di Santos had arrived on the touchline – and he was livid for some reason.

"What are you doing, Boy? Make the tackle!"

Distracted by his insane manager barking orders at him, Charlie paused.

He was unsure whether to press the defender as his manager wanted, or drop back to keep his position – as instinct told him to.

His hesitation proved costly.

Ben raced into the space behind him as Charlie finally decided to make the tackle a fraction too late.

The full-back waited for the Boy Wonder to close in before he released an angled pass into Ben's path, easily avoiding Charlie's lunge.

Hulcote were away again – and this time there would be no mistake.

In acres of room Ben curled an inviting cross right on to the head of the Hulcote striker.

Charlie caught up with Ben moments too late and they both watched as the forward headed the ball firmly towards Hall Park's net.

Joe moved to his right but had no chance.

The keeper's despairing dive was not enough as the ball flew into the top corner.

Hall Park Rovers 0, Hulcote United 1.

The game was only four minutes old and Charlie was worried his body could collapse at any moment.

Exhausted, he was seeing stars and barely able to speak as he stumbled back to his position.

He would not last the full match – particularly as all the focus seemed to be on him. His body could not cope.

Wiping away the snot streaming from his nose, Charlie bent over double as Joe booted the ball back to the centre circle for the restart.

As Charlie stood there, a familiar cold voice sounded in his ear.

"Boy. I'm not sure if you're an idiot or just lazy. That goal was your fault.

"You are a disgrace, Fry. If you ever dare to ignore my orders again then you'll be sorry – Boy Wonder or not."

Charlie did not even look at Di Santos or show any sign he'd heard his threats. He was fed up of this golden boy manager and his bullying.

Hall Park restarted the game and Bishop immediately pinged the ball to Charlie who, despite being barely able to stand, somehow managed to pass back to Seamus.

A long aimless punt forward followed and gave possession straight back to the away team.

Once more Hulcote's right-back was given the ball – another attack was about to come down Charlie's side.

Shattered from the long warm-up and the frenetic start to the match, Charlie found himself two-on-one yet again.

"FRY! TO HIM! NOW!

This time Charlie didn't pause.

He moved as fast as he could towards the Hulcote defender and ignored his body's screams of unhappiness.

Charlie's movement cut off the simple pass to Ben and forced the right-back to pass back to his 'keeper.

Unfortunately, the goalie then simply clipped a long ball back over Charlie's head towards the Hulcote winger.

Charlie turned and saw Ben was completely free – again. The new formation meant he was being constantly outnumbered.

"BOY! THIS IS YOUR MAN! WHAT ARE YOU DOING?"

Spit flew from Chell Di Santos's lips as he raged at Charlie, who was now way out of position and miles behind the play.

But another voice could be heard on the touchline now.

"Oi! Who do you think you are? This is a kids' football match! You leave him alone – you are a pathetic bully."

Joe's mum Steffi had seen enough and could no longer hold back her fury as she marched towards the Hall Park boss.

His eyes alive with fury, Di Santos broke away from the game to face the angry parent in front of him.

His voice was dangerously low.

"Shut up, you stupid idiot. This is my team. Keep

your views to yourself."

Steffi laughed loudly: "Perhaps I should take over then, you moron.

"You told Charlie to close the man down, and then shout at him for being up the pitch! He may be the Boy Wonder but he's not Superman."

As they began arguing in front of everyone, the game kept going.

Ben accelerated into the Hall Park half with the ball at his feet and approached Joe's goal without anyone making a tackle.

Charlie did not see the Hulcote winger hit a blistering swerving shot with the outside of his right foot.

And he missed Joe getting a hand to the thunderbolt.

Nor did he witness the ball strike the inside of the post and drop agonisingly just over the line for Hulcote's second goal in as many minutes.

Hall Park Rovers 0, Hulcote United 2.

The Boy Wonder was on his knees next to the side-line. Charlie felt horrendous, his body pushed to its limit.

He could not run another step.

Exhaustion was upon him.

As he began to vomit on the pitch in front of shocked fans, a familiar icy whisper appeared in his ear again.

"You're weak, Fry. You're pathetic. You are selfish, you think football is all about you. It's about a team, not a Boy Wonder.

"I was told you were a great player. We now know that's not true don't we? You play for yourself, no one else.

"I gave you your big chance and you've blown it. Say bye to Hall Park because …"

Di Santos did not get the chance to finish his sentence.

Liam Fry had watched from the stands as his eldest son was run into the ground by this lunatic but his patience had run out.

The beefy builder grabbed the startled manager around the neck and tossed him straight into the ice bucket holding the team's half-time drinks.

Liam was a man of few words.

Eyes blazing he towered over the stunned football manager, who struggled to remove himself from the freezing water container.

"Never speak to my son … ever again."

Charlie felt his dad's strong arms lift him up as a soaked Di Santos finally managed to get free from the bucket.

As his dad carried him towards the changing room, Charlie could hear the stadium announcer: "Six minutes gone and it's the first substitution of the game. Charlie Fry for.…"

His big match had lasted just six awful minutes.

21. END OF A DREAM

Charlie sat on the couch waiting for his parents to return from their meeting with Hall Park's senior committee.

Joe and Peter were perched on the two armchairs opposite as they discussed the Hulcote game that happened the day before.

Charlie had recovered after the sickness but his cold was getting worse. He expected to go into hospital in the next day or so.

He had barely moved from the couch since getting home. He knew he'd been foolish but he was adamant that he'd had no choice.

After Charlie's early substitution, Hall Park had turned things around to win 5-2 in style – but only after they switched back to their usual 4-4-2 formation.

The three of them were certain about one thing: the surprise change in formation was a sneaky trick by Di Santos designed to make Charlie run further than anyone else on the team.

It all added up.

The extra-long warm-up, the new formation, the taunts about his lack of fitness and effort from the side-line all seemed to be part of a nasty plan.

But why would he do that?

Surely football managers want to have the best players in their team?

Peter had his own theory on that.

In his mind Di Santos was the real star.

He needed to be the person who was loved and adored by the crowd and media.

His teams in the past – when he had managed abroad – were successful but never produced any stars.

That's because he did not share the limelight.

And having a striker named The Boy Wonder was never going to work with a manager like that.

Charlie and Joe did not disagree with him. It did make sense.

Joe was keeping particularly quiet about the manager – his mum's huge row with Di Santos during the Hulcote game had resulted in him being dropped to the bench for the next game.

To say the goalkeeper was annoyed was an understatement.

Charlie felt bad for his friend – he had never meant for any of this to happen.

And it wasn't only the Rovers players that had fallen foul of the demon football manager.

The Telegraph had been banned from future matches – after asking too many questions about the early substitution of Charlie.

Di Santos was now putting his stamp on Hall Park Academy set-up in all sorts of different ways.

Nonetheless, his Under-13s team was unbeaten in the first three games of the season so far and were in second place in the league.

His unusual management technique seemed to bring results.

The form of Rovers could not have been different to Peter's team: Magpies had been thrashed 13-1 at home by Aztec.

Peter, who was now nearly fully fit, had gloomily recounted the match to his friends, explaining a lack of players had cost the Hall Park second string dearly.

"We've got people leaving us, left, right and centre. Dazza quit last night.

"No-one likes playing for a team that gets hammered every week. Sometimes we have enough for a starting 11 but not every game."

It was unfair. They felt for Peter and the other Magpies players. Being thrashed every week was not fun.

Peter continued: "We have got good players but what chance have we got when we're starting matches with only nine players against 11?

"We might be relegated before I make my debut at this rate!"

The boys' conversation stopped abruptly as they heard a car door slamming shut on the driveway.

Charlie's parents were back.

It was the moment of truth.

Unseen by the others Charlie crossed his fingers underneath his leg as Liam and Molly came into the house through the front door.

He looked at his parents' faces and knew instantly it was bad news.

Charlie mustered the courage to ask the question.

His voice came out clearly but wavered a tad, showing his nerves.

"Dad, how did it go?"

Liam bit his lip, his tone gentle but direct as always.

"Not good, Son. They were very nice and wished you luck in the future but...."

His dad's voice tailed off, unable to find the right words.

Charlie switched to his mum, fearing what the next sentence would contain.

She moved closer to her boy, pulling him into a tight hug.

"I'm sorry, Charlie. The manager has been adamant over this and has requested permission to release you from Hall Park."

"No!" Joe and Peter cried together.

Silence fell upon the room before Charlie's dad spoke up again.

"I'm sorry, Son. Chell Di Santos has won.

"You're not a Hall Park Rovers player any more. It's over."

EPILOGUE

Golden leaves flew across the path as the chilly autumn wind lashed the Crickledon Rec.

Charlie soldiered on against the blustery gales heading home.

Both Joe and Peter had football training so he was making the long trek back from school alone.

Apart from a few dog walkers, the awful weather made sure the park was virtually empty.

Winter was coming.

It had been three weeks since his shock axing from Hall Park.

Charlie had spent ten days in hospital recovering from his cold and had just returned to school.

Things had changed.

He was no longer the school celebrity.

Instead he was now the subject of playground gossip, silly whispers and more than a few horrible taunts.

The cries of "Boy Wonder" had turned into "Sick Boy" in the space of a month.

Fame was fickle, Peter had said wisely.

Luckily Charlie was used to idiot bullies and blanked them as best he could.

It hurt though to think he was no longer a Hall Park Rovers striker.

Charlie Fry was now an ex-footballer – and he hadn't even had his twelfth birthday yet.

He could not believe what had happened. The target was still floating randomly round his vision as always, now barely used.

Charlie tried his best to ignore it.

The lightning bolt, the magic target, the Boy Wonder banners, the glory goals, the incredible newspaper reports – it seemed like a world away already.

Rovers had won their next two games comfortably without him.

Chell Di Santos was being feted as the next Jose Mourinho by the media – except by the Telegraph whose reporter was still banned from Hall Park games.

Charlie was pleased for the lads.

Bishop was banging the goals in and Joe had won his place back after his one-match punishment on the bench.

But how could all these people not see Di Santos for what he was?

He was a nasty bully and nothing more.

Charlie nestled a little deeper into his coat as he reached the park gates, preparing for the final leg of the journey home.

As he left the park, he was approached by a familiar face.

Annie Cooper was in his science class.

Petite with long brown hair, Annie was always smiling and joking. Everyone thought she was great.

And she loved football.

She had turned out for Magpies a couple of times this season already – and Peter couldn't have been higher in her praise.

"A proper player," was how Belly described her.

"All right Boy Wonder?" Annie flashed Charlie her winning smile.

"Don't call me that, Annie."

Charlie, who was beginning to hate that nickname, kept walking eager to get out of the cold.

"Okay, okay," replied Annie as she fell in alongside him. "I've got someone who wants to talk to you."

Charlie stopped and looked at her.

They were nearly the same size. She wore a red headband and had a sprinkle of cute freckles across her nose.

"Who?"

The door of a car parked nearby opened and they both turned to face the person who got out and walked towards them.

"Hello Charlie."

Charlie was amazed Johnny Cooper knew his name.

Suddenly he felt awkward.

"Er, hello."

Johnny smiled and put arm around Annie.

"You've met my daughter then?"

Charlie gawped at Coops, switched his gaze to Annie and then back to the professional footballer standing in front of him.

"Wait, you're his … er, yes, we have science together."

Coops lazily pushed a hand through his long blonde hair and grinned.

"So I've heard. How would you like to have football together too?"

Charlie tilted his head. He did not understand what Coops meant.

The man smiled at Charlie's confusion.

"Let me spell it out. How do you fancy being signed by Magpies?"

Charlie smiled weakly but shook his head.

"I can't. My dad has already suggested that idea to the Hall Park committee but they said I could no longer represent any Hall Park team."

And, after a moment's hesitation, Charlie added: "I'm finished."

Coops moved forward and put a hand on Charlie's shoulder.

"No, Boy Wonder, you're wrong. You've not even started yet.

"And you're far too good for Hall Park to give up on, no matter what that moronic Rovers manager says."

Charlie could feel himself stand a little taller, thrilled that other people didn't think too much of Di Santos either.

He was yet to be convinced though.

"But...."

Annie interrupted immediately.

"There's no 'but' here, Charlie.

"Do you really think that Hall Park will ignore what my dad says? He's the best player they have EVER had at the club.

"His opinion matters.

"And, luckily for you, he thinks you're pretty

special so he's stuck his neck out for you."

Coops put a hand up to halt Annie's words.

"I'm not sure I would have put it quite like that but Coops junior has a point.

"I have spoken in person to the committee and they have agreed to allow you to become a Magpies player – if you wish to return.

"What do you say?"

Barely able to believe what was happening, Charlie's heart flipped with excitement and his hand shot out to accept the offer.

"Is … this … for … real?!" Charlie stammered.

Coops laughed as he eased Charlie's hand away from his.

"Yes, Boy Wonder.

"You can dream about being a top footballer again.

"I know you won't let me down.

"Go again, and remember to show them all – especially that demon football manager – exactly how good the Football Boy Wonder truly is."

A SNEAK PEEK

Thank you for reading The Demon Football Manager – the second instalment in the Charlie Fry Series.

I hope you've enjoyed Charlie's tale so far.

Please leave your feedback and reviews on Amazon – it is gratefully received.

I'm busy writing the next part of Charlie's adventure and am hoping to publish the third book in the Charlie Fry series soon.

To whet your appetite, here's an exclusive look at the first chapter of the third Charlie Fry series – The Magic Football Book.

Enjoy and, again, thank you for reading.

**

Manor Park was a gloomy place even on a hot summer day.

In the middle of a cold and wet November, it was truly grim.

It was Crickledon's smallest park – and home to

the Hall Park Magpies' Under-13s team.

A children's play area with half the equipment broken or missing stood in one corner while a derelict skate park occupied the opposite end.

Between them was a football pitch that had its grass cut once every few weeks when the groundskeeper had five minutes to spare.

Next to the pitch stood the park's clubhouse with almost every centimetre of the building's wooden walls covered in graffiti.

Charlie Fry stood next to his dad at the Manor Park gates looking at the unlikely place he was hoping to revive his football career.

Manor Park was popular with town's wannabe footballers because it had nets attached to its goalposts all year round.

No-one ever bothered to take them down.

The nets were ancient too with holes easily big enough for the ball to escape through, hanging off rusted goalposts.

The FA had stopped Magpies playing at the Hall Park stadium – insisting that too many teams were already playing there.

It meant Magpies had been forced to find somewhere else and Manor Park was the only realistic option.

It was not pretty but it was a home for the team and that was the main thing.

A small group of Magpies players gently warmed up at the edge of the pitch.

"What are they doing?"

Charlie pointed at several people wearing gloves, bending down and scooping up parts of the pitch into carrier bags.

His buddy Peter Bell piped up behind them.

"Dog owners let their pets do their mess all over the park.

"Some clean up after them, others don't.

"We can't play with dog poop everywhere so Magpies' players, parents and coaches take turns to clear the pitches before training and matches.

"We all take a turn – that's how it works at Magpies. We all chip in."

Things were certainly different here to Rovers, Charlie thought to himself, as Peter slapped him with glee on the shoulder.

His friend was fit enough to play football again – months after Adam Knight had broken his leg in the summer Hall Park trials.

It seemed like a lifetime ago now.

Peter was buzzing – he was finally on a football pitch again and would soon line up alongside his best friend again.

Charlie was happy for Belly but was nervous about the way the rest of the team would treat him.

He knew almost every one of the group – but had not spoken with many of them since Rovers and Magpies had been divided up into separate teams several months ago.

The Boy Wonder walked slowly down the slope towards the circle of players with his dad and Peter, chewing his lip with apprehension.

Before they reached the group, Peter shouted: "Mapgies, here's our new boy.

"The Football Boy Wonder himself – Mr Charlie Fry!"

Shocked at his friend's unexpected outburst, Charlie blushed furiously.

He simply wanted to be one of the team, not treated like a superstar.

With all the newspaper stories and banners, he'd had enough of that nonsense.

He did not need to worry.

The team obviously listened to Peter – and the cheering was loud and genuine.

Before he knew it, they were chanting: "We're not going down, we're not going down...."

Charlie smiled at the friendly welcome as one of the crowd stepped forward.

It was Annie, dressed in the all-yellow Magpies kit with her long brown hair pushed back into a ponytail.

She was holding a bright orange ball under her arm and grinned at the Boy Wonder before she booted the ball high in the air.

As everyone watched the ball fly high into the sky, Annie yelled: "Come on then, Fry.

"Show us some skills and remind us what all the fuss is about!"

Charlie didn't need another invite.

He dropped his kitbag and watched the ball rocket up into the dark sky.

He ran into the space where he anticipated it would come back down before he flicked his eyes towards the empty goal.

The target inside his mind, inactive for so long, responded immediately.

It flew straight to the net in Charlie's vision and flashed green instantly.

It took a split second – Charlie had lost none of skill with the magic ability from that lucky lightning bolt.

The ball had begun to fall rapidly out of the sky as

Charlie returned his full concentration to it.

He met the ball on the half volley and timed the connection perfectly.

The sweetly struck shot rocketed towards the goal and even skimmed the top of the Magpies manager's head as it flew into the empty net without a single bounce.

"Oi!

"Mr Fry!"

Charlie winced.

Had he really managed to upset Barney Payne, the Magpies' boss, already?

Was the Chell Di Santos nightmare about to begin again?

Charlie held his breath as Barney, who had been busy scooping up dog poo into a carrier bag, shouted over to him.

"What on earth are you doing, Charlie?

"Save that kind of thing for the matches!

"Don't go wasting wonderful skill like that in training!"

Charlie realised Barney was smiling along with the other coaches.

Annie walked up to him and hugged him, making Charlie blush.

"About time! Welcome to Magpies, Mr Football Boy Wonder."

Barney hadn't quite finished with him yet though.

He walked up to the newcomers, nodded to Charlie's dad Liam and Peter before talking to Charlie again: "Yes, yes, yes. Welcome to the Magpies, Mr Fry.

"And when you've quite finished with the display of World Cup-winning skill, there's a big pile of dog poo over here with your name on it!"

Charlie smiled as he took the poop scoop from the manager.

He felt at home already.

**

Charlie's story continues in The Magic Football Book – available from Amazon today.

ABOUT THE AUTHOR

Martin Smith lives in Northamptonshire with his wife and daughter.

He has spent more than 15 years working in the UK's regional press before moving into the internal communication industry.

He has cystic fibrosis, diagnosed with the condition as a two-year-old.

The Charlie Fry series is not autobiographical (Martin has never been a footballing great or struck by a lightning bolt, as far as he recalls) but certainly some aspects are based on real life.

Hall Park, for example, has witnessed some of the greatest football matches the world has ever seen.

The Charlie Fry series is about friendship, self-belief and a love of football – the one sport that seems to unite people of all backgrounds under one cause.

Thanks for reading.

And always, always believe.

ALSO BY MARTIN SMITH

THE FOOTBALL BOY WONDER

Charlie Fry is football mad.

He plays football around the clock – at the park, on the way to school, at lunchtimes, and even in his bedroom – until his mum tells him off.

But Charlie had a problem: he can't run very far. He has plenty of skill but his poorly lungs stop him from sprinting.

And as a 11-year-old planning to become the Golden Boot Winner at a future World Cup, that's an issue.

Then one day a freak accident presents Charlie with a unique goal-scoring gift – he can't miss.

But can Charlie convince his local team Hall Park to give him the chance to use his new skill to deadly effect?

Or will the nasty bullies from his school keep him stuck on the sidelines?

The Football Boy Wonder is available via Amazon and the Kindle store today.

Printed in Poland
by Amazon Fulfillment
Poland Sp. z o.o., Wrocław